I Want You As My Woman.

Demi forced herself to breathe; Rafe's words stunned her. Discovering her own sensuality and the Tallchief legend that applied to Rafe had unnerved her. She wanted time to consider the legend and adapt to the new woman emerging in her—one who wanted Rafe and everything that love entailed. One with her own dreams, not those of other people. Her need for Rafe—ill-tempered as he was now—overrode her desire to please anyone else, including him.

She couldn't love him.

But there it was—stark, humming, heating, flowing between them, a mix of tenderness, desire, the need to give and take. Everything she craved in a man was here, now, with Rafe, a man who was her opposite.

Life would not flow easily with Rafe.

Dear Reader,

August predictably brings long steamy days...and hot sensuous nights. And this month Silhouette Desire spotlights the kind of pure passion that can erupt only in that sizzling summer climate.

Get ready to fall head over heels for August's MAN OF THE MONTH, a sexy rancher who opens his home (and his heart?) to a lost beauty desperately hoping to recover her memory in *A Montana Man* by Jackie Merritt. Bestselling author Cait London continues her hugely popular miniseries THE TALLCHIEFS with *Rafe Palladin: Man of Secrets*. Rafe is an irresistible takeover tycoon with a plan to *acquire* a Tallchief lady. Barbara McMahon brings readers the second story in her IDENTICAL TWINS! duo—in *The Older Man* an exuberant young woman is swept up by her love and desire for a tremendously gorgeous, *much* older man.

Plus, talented Susan Crosby unfolds a story of seduction, revenge and scandal in the continuation of THE LONE WOLVES with *His Seductive Revenge*. And TEXAS BRIDES are back with *The Restless Virgin* by Peggy Moreland, the story of an innocent Western lady tired of waiting around for marriage—so she lassos herself one unsuspecting cowboy! And you've never seen a hero like *The Consummate Cowboy,* by Sara Orwig. He's all man, all-around ornery and all-out tempted...by his ex-wife's sister!

I know you'll enjoy reading all six of this sultry month's brand-new Silhouette Desire novels by some of the most beloved and sexy authors of romance.

Regards,

Melissa Senate

Melissa Senate
Senior Editor
Silhouette Books

Please address questions and book requests to:
Silhouette Reader Service
U.S.: 3010 Walden Ave., P.O. Box 1325, Buffalo, NY 14269
Canadian: P.O. Box 609, Fort Erie, Ont. L2A 5X3

CAIT
LONDON
RAFE PALLADIN:
MAN OF SECRETS

SILHOUETTE *Desire*

Published by Silhouette Books

America's Publisher of Contemporary Romance

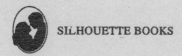

SILHOUETTE BOOKS

ISBN 0-373-76160-0

RAFE PALLADIN: MAN OF SECRETS

Printed in U.S.A.

Books by Cait London

Silhouette Desire

*The Loving Season #502
*Angel vs. MacLean #593
The Pendragon Virus #611
*The Daddy Candidate #641
†Midnight Rider #726
The Cowboy #763
Maybe No, Maybe Yes #782
†The Seduction of Jake Tallman #811
Fusion #871
The Bride Says No #891
Mr. Easy #919
Miracles and Mistletoe #968
‡The Cowboy and the Cradle #1006
‡Tallchief's Bride #1021
‡The Groom Candidate #1093
‡The Seduction of Fiona Tallchief #1135
‡Rafe Palladin: Man of Secrets #1160

*The MacLeans
†The Blaylocks
‡The Tallchiefs

Silhouette Yours Truly

Every Girl's Guide To...
Every Groom's Guide To...

Silhouette Books

‡Tallchief for Keeps

Spring Fancy 1994
"Lightfoot and Loving"

CAIT LONDON

lives in the Missouri Ozarks but loves to travel the Northwest's gold rush/cattle drive trails every summer. She loves research trips, meeting people and going to Native American dances. Ms. London is an avid reader who loves to paint, play with computers and grow herbs (particularly scented geraniums right now). She's a national bestselling and award-winning author, and she also writes historical romances under another pseudonym. Three is her lucky number; she has three daughters, and the events in her life have always been in threes. "I love writing for Silhouette," she says. "One of the best perks about all this hard work is the thrilling reader response and the warm, snug sense that I have given readers an enjoyable, entertaining gift."

To those who enjoy Greek mythology as much as I do,
and to my marvelous editors at Silhouette,
Melissa and Isabel.

'Twil be the knight who brings his lady to this cave with clusters of crystals about—aye, the sparkling crystals shall shoot their cloak of colors about him, who loves her already. Rogue that he is, the lady will come to love him with all her heart.

One

"A moat and a closed drawbridge. Just what every castle in Wyoming needs," Rafe murmured as he stood overlooking the small valley shrouded in snowflakes.

February wind sliced at his face, tore at his expensive English woolen coat and hurled it around him like a black cape. He ignored the wind's icy bite sinking through his three-piece tailored gray suit and the snowflakes settling upon his hair and shoulders. A man with a mission, he locked his custom-made Italian shoes to the snow-covered ground. He bent to retrieve his binoculars from the seat of his pearl gray BMW, lifting them to view the ill-kept castle his father had sold to Dr. Nathaniel Valerian.

Nestled close to the soaring Rocky Mountains, and overseeing a small valley, the tiny castle looked out of place, surrounded by pine forests and the background of jutting, snow-covered mountains.

On the other side of a small mountain rested Amen Flats, the home of the Tallchiefs. Joel, Rafe's older brother, had married

Fiona Tallchief and if Rafe hurried to complete the transaction his grandmother wanted so badly, he could spend time with Joel's family.

Rafe tugged up the collar of his coat, leaned against his BMW and dropped into his thoughts. Acquiring the castle and soothing the conscience of his grandmother, who felt guilty for her son's crimes, would be an easy task. Mamie Palladin wanted Dr. Valerian well repaid for the folly he had purchased from her son: the small castle that had plunged the Valerians into debt and was sucking Dr. Valerian's health.

Rafe smoothed his latest mechanical pet's expensive pearl gray finish. In this country, a four-wheeler would have served better than the BMW, but he enjoyed the luxury, a contrast to his early years.

Rafe found the small crystal attached to the key ring in his pocket. As a boy, he had discovered it years ago in the same castle, and for some reason he'd kept it as a talisman.

The Valerians, father and daughter, would probably leap at having the castle taken off their hands—and the handsome profit. As chief of Palladin, Inc.'s acquisitions and product development, Rafe had the quick-claim deed in his briefcase, ready to be signed. He'd follow Mamie's orders, though it went against his nature to give money away. Rafe had teethed on darker elements than charity.

He scanned the low clouds blanketing the mountains and laden with snow. With his grandmother, Mamie, and his brothers, Joel and Nick, Rafe had been trying to set right their father's crimes and scams.

Lloyd Palladin's schemes had ended in a life sentence for murder, and he'd been killed in prison. He'd given his sons nothing, not even pride. They'd built that with Mamie's help. His grandmother had jerked her grandsons from the streets, shoved them into decent clothing and rules and manners, despite their fighting every inch of the way.

Rafe ran his hand through his neatly clipped hair, surprised at the fine trembling. He studied his hands, neatly manicured but big and tough like his father's. Hell, all the Palladin sons looked like Lloyd: dark brown hair, green eyes and a cleft in the center of their chins.

He felt as lonely and out of place as the tiny castle yanked from English soil and hurled, stone by stone, into the Rocky Mountains. The last twenty-four hours had torn Rafe apart. His mother's letter, written years earlier, had been sent by a friend of hers, and last week Rafe had discovered that Belinda was not his biological mother.

Joel and Nick were not his full brothers.

"The bastard of the family." Rafe braced himself against the fresh pain as though a piece of him had been torn away and tossed into the icy winds. Belinda's letter had been written after the birth of Nick, the youngest Palladin, almost thirty-three years earlier. Six months later, she had died.

Belinda had wanted to protect him and he was the only one to know that his biological mother was a terrified fourteen-year-old girl whom Lloyd Palladin had raped. Not even Lloyd knew that Rafe was not her child; Belinda, a loving woman, had known what Lloyd would do to a son he did not want to claim. She had padded her body and since Lloyd was absent most of their marriage, she had merely presented him with another son upon his return.

In her letter, forgotten in a bank vault for years, Belinda had worried that Rafe might want to find his real mother.

Through everything—Belinda's early death, his father's brutality and schemes—all Rafe had ever had was the knowledge that the three Palladin sons were a unit—strong, invincible, building their pride from nothing.

And now, he wasn't one of them.

"Hold. Who goes there?" a man called out as a fresh blast of icy wind whipped around Rafe. Though it was only five o'clock, the cold mountain night shielded the castle now, and Rafe stood in front of his headlights, making his identification easier.

"Rafe Palladin, representing Palladin, Inc." He hurled his voice into the wind and checked his wristwatch. If he hurried, he could be at Joel's house—not far from Amen Flats—for dinner. Joel and Fiona's new baby, Ian, was just four and a half months old, and when Rafe held him... He brushed away the thought; he wasn't certain what emotions Ian called forth, other than the fascination that he was tiny and perfect.

Rafe glanced out into the shadows, remembering when his father had brought him and his brothers here, to patch the castle, "pretty it up," to sell it. Joel, Nick and Rafe were too young to do the men's work their father demanded. He had ridiculed them into doing it, covering rotten boards with new ones, sweeping out the clutter of pack rats, scrubbing the windows. Rafe had been badly cut, too young to use a power saw. To save a doctor bill, Lloyd had cauterized the wound with a knife's hot steel. So much for tenderness.

At night, while their father drank steadily, the brothers had lain on the floor and dreamed of being knights, protecting the castle and all who lived within. He'd held the crystal to the light, lost himself in the myriad of colors bursting from it and dreamed of the princess that he would rescue one day.

Rafe kicked aside a small clump of snow. His dreams were gone; perhaps they never were. He functioned as he had to, for Mamie's sake.

Rafe frowned as the drawbridge began to lower, chains creaking. He'd been a part of his father's scam, taking Dr. Valerian's retirement and his savings.

"Enter and welcome. Will you sup with us, friend?" the man asked cheerfully as the heavy planks of the drawbridge slammed into the ground. "Did you say, 'Palladin'? I bought this wonderful castle from a Palladin."

"I'm his son." Rafe forced the admission. He went back to the car to turn off his headlights, and pick up his briefcase. As he made his way across the safe parts of the drawbridge, a rotted board tumbled down into the moat, filled with snow and debris.

"I'm Dr. Nathaniel Valerian. Welcome to my humble home, my castle, so to speak." Nathaniel was painfully thin, balding, dressed in light slacks, house slippers and a worn sweater over his shirt. He clutched an old book against him and looked through his small round glasses up the distance to Rafe's face. He lifted the lantern higher. "You look like him. The exact image. The same towering height—six-two or so, am I correct? How is my friend, Lloyd Palladin?"

"Deceased. I am six-two." Rafe saw no reason to examine Lloyd's road to prison, the murder of the Tallchiefs' parents, which had left five children to fend for themselves. Joel had married the youngest, Fiona Tallchief, and Rafe intended to visit them—or would he? Belinda's letter, once revealed, could shatter more lives. Had Belinda left other letters for Joel and Nick?

"I'm sorry. He was a good man. He let me have this castle at a steal, because he knew how important it was to me. I had tracked its authenticity and have proof that Montclair hunting lodge was actually transported across the Atlantic at the turn of the century. It took five years for Sir Niles Montclair to accomplish his mission, but just look—" Nathaniel surveyed the castle with pride. "It took over twenty years to take possession of this wonderful castle...to move in. I dreamed of it every moment from the down payment on the loan, until my retirement. Look what Sir Niles accomplished—placing the Montclair castle directly within the very mountains that Liam Tallchief and Liam's full-blood Sioux father, Tallchief, roamed and hunted. Liam and Elizabeth Montclair Tallchief had three children, one of which was my grandmother. She married a Valerian."

An expert at studying people in business deals, Rafe braced himself against the price of the castle, which sentimentality had just raised. He thought of his sleek, comfortable penthouse in Denver, and the Palladin ranch house, which was appropriately luxurious for Mamie. His grandmother liked the sprawling ranch, but when needing isolation to transact difficult business, she wanted all the luxuries possible for her guests. Rafe would stay at the ranch, managing it as he always had, until he resolved how to handle his relationships with Joel and Nick and Mamie.

Mamie. Spry and in her eighties, she wanted to ease her conscience about her son's wrongs. Rafe wondered briefly how she would feel about him—the black sheep of the family. Then, with the experience of a man who let little interfere with his life, he turned his mind to the challenge before him. "You got my letter then—that Palladin, Inc. would like to purchase the castle?"

Nathaniel sneezed lightly as he led the way to the double wooden door, the heavy planks patched with odd boards. They angled haphazardly, resembling a child's attempt to apply adhesive bandages. "The doors are stuck. We haven't been able to open them since the freezing weather, but we're quite able to come and go through the kitchen door," Nathaniel said, and drew Rafe to a smaller side door. "I hope you won't mind coming into the kitchen—"

"Father!" A woman's indignant tone hurtled at them as he opened the door. A woman who barely reached Rafe's chest and wore a circlet of gleaming black braids on top of her head hurried to Nathaniel with a woolen shawl, draping it around his thin shoulders. She drew him into the kitchen. "Father, just look at your feet. How many times have I told you to wear your boots when going out in the snow?" she demanded, then glared at Rafe over the tops of her round glasses as if he were the culprit who had caused Nathaniel to misbehave.

"Come in, young man, and have sup with us. My daughter is a wonderful cook, but she worries overmuch," Nathaniel offered as Rafe tried to push the door shut, blocking out the freezing winds. The door refused to move until Rafe placed his shoulder against the wood and pushed it closed.

Nathaniel nodded. "Yes, you are as powerful as your father. I see that. Both physical men—"

"I am very different from my father," Rafe stated abruptly. He'd worked to build his pride.

"And who are you?" the woman demanded in a tone that matched the bitter, freezing weather outside the kitchen.

Dr. Valerian smiled fondly. "My daughter, Demi Tallchief. After her divorce she reclaimed an ancestorial name, which has made me very proud. A Tallchief residing in a Montclair castle only seems right. Perhaps you've heard of the Tallchiefs of Amen Flats. We are distant cousins and have recently made their acquaintance. She prefers Demi to Demeter, which is goddess of the harvest. Are you familiar with Greek mythology, Mr. Palladin?"

"Call me Rafe. I'm afraid I've never had time to study mythology." Rafe saw no reason to chitchat about his own new relatives, the Tallchiefs. In his experience, a business deal was better without charity and friendship. From the way the woman hovered around her father, she was more the parent than child. According to Rafe's preacquisition research, Demi was thirty-one and divorced. She would have influence on Valerian's decision to sell the castle, and Rafe would have to find her weaknesses.

The woman was dressed shapelessly in a huge, patched apron which covered a man's sweater and draped past her hips, a long woolen skirt, black stockings and practical, worn brogans with knots repairing the shoelaces. The light from inside gleamed on her braided raven hair, wound tightly on top of her head. Though shorter and stockier built than the towering Tallchief family, Demi had the sleek black hair of the Sioux chieftain, Tallchief, and the searing, stormy gray eyes of his Scots captive bride, Una.

The Tallchief pride was there, locked in her flushed cheeks, her lifted chin, her straight shoulders and her feet braced upon the castle stones.

Rafe had seen his first Tallchief when attending the Tallchief parents' private funeral on Tallchief Mountain. He and his brothers, teenage sons of the murderer, had taken the bus with the last of their money, determined to pay their respects. But Fiona Tallchief had run them off the mountain. Now, Fiona was married to Joel, and the Tallchiefs—Duncan, Calum, Elspeth, Birk and Fiona—had welcomed the Palladins into their family.

But Rafe didn't belong with either family; the letter from Belinda had placed a wedge between Joel, Nick and himself. Kept safely by Belinda's aging friend, the letter had been filled with brief, cruel realities and with loving passages, proving Belinda's love for her children. Belinda had worried that one day, Rafe's real mother may need him desperately and that he should know. *She had loved Rafe, cared enough to deceive the world and treat him as though he were her son, the same as Nick and Joel.* He wondered how he would tell them; they had survived together and now— Who was his real mother? Was she alive?

"Palladin?" Demi asked, her black eyebrows lifting. Her gray eyes seemed to smoke, narrowing threateningly at Rafe. "The man who wrote the letter, and the acquisitions director of Palladin, Inc.? *The son of the swindler?*" With each word, her outrage deepened and Rafe noted that she had not used the word, "murderer."

Rafe stripped his Italian kidskin gloves from him, saw the big scarred, tough hands resembling his father's and braced himself against the condemning, familiar word. The sons of Lloyd Palladin had teethed on their dark legacy.

"Demi! You know that we're lucky to have this wonderful castle. It is a part of your heritage."

The pride and ownership in Nathaniel's voice took the price Palladin would pay a notch higher. A man experienced at sorting visions of success from cold reality, Rafe scanned the spotless kitchen: a small fire burned in an open stone hearth, a kettle hung from a rod over the flickering flames, a battered refrigerator. A teakettle hissed on an old electric stove. The lid of a slow cooker released steam, suggesting its use, and bread waited to be removed from the pans. An old sewing machine and fabrics littered one corner by a window and herbs hung in bundles from a rack made of trimmed branches. Squashes and pumpkins were stacked in a basket; shelves lined the walls, filled with canned foods and jars of beans and grains. A washer with a coin slot chugged in another corner; the electrical cord running from a main outlet to the machine looked frayed, as if it could burst into flame in a second.

A table that Rafe remembered being covered with rats and litter sat near another window, lined with battered chairs that he doubted would hold his two hundred pounds. Everything in the room, including the worn scatter rugs, was painfully shabby and clean. Yet the soft touches caused the room to look cheery and warm, unlike the woman's steel gray eyes, which had never left Rafe.

He turned slowly to her and met her cold stare.

A man who had battled for his pride, Rafe disliked her accusing glare down her straight nose and over her glasses. The shade of her eyes reminded him briefly of a stormy sky reflected in his crystal. She folded her arms protectively over her chest. "My father said we're not selling, and that is final."

Her voice, though clipped and furious, held softer tones, a feminine husky tone that snagged at Rafe. "I thought a personal visit and discussion might better—"

"No. Since you have no further business here, you may go." Demi glanced worriedly at her father, who had just sneezed again. "Father, did you take your medicine?"

He looked at her absently, and glanced at the clock. "It's past four. Yes, I must have. Please, dear. I insist you calm yourself and be gracious to our visitor."

Rafe studied Demi Tallchief. Though she might not be familiar with the "stand and fight" motto of the Tallchiefs, she was not making his visit easy. What would she want? Other than money? What would induce her to sell?

She shot Rafe a look that said "friendly" wasn't on her list of how to treat him, then she hurried to a chart taped to a rock wall. She smoothed her hands on her large apron. "You did not place a check by four o'clock, Father. Eight o'clock, twelve o'clock, but there is no four o'clock," she underlined. "You know how important it is to keep up the dosage for your cough."

"Oh, dear." Nathaniel's slow smile made him seem years younger. "My daughter worries about me. She's prepared a lovely beef stew, nourishing, you know. The Tallchiefs—lovely people with a beautiful heritage—own cattle, you know—gave us a welcoming gift of several packages of frozen meat. We don't have a freezer, but heavens, with winter around, who needs more than a box safely secured outside the attic rooms."

"Mr. Palladin can't stay," Demi said firmly. She crossed the room to pour hot water from the pot on the fire into an English teapot; she covered it with a worn, daisy-splashed cozy. "He's had his answer and he's leaving."

Rafe disliked anyone pushing him; he'd had enough of it when he was younger. A man experienced with shielding his emotions and controlling them, he met Demi's fierce stare with a mild smile. "Thank you, Dr. Valerian, for the offer of dinner. Later, if you have time, I'd love to see the rest of the castle, just to see what Palladin, Inc. is missing."

"It's just a castle, like every other castle," Demi stated briskly. "You know, the everyday, generic four turrets, parapets, ramparts, towers. The barracks and chapel are really only small rooms. The dining hall and great room are just a main hall—it was really a hunting lodge. If you've seen one, you've seen 'em all. No antlers, of course. I couldn't bear the dead animal parts hanging about and Father is allergic to animals."

Demi's eagerness for Rafe to leave only made him more determined to stay. "I've always loved English history," he said slowly, and enjoyed the sudden widening of her eyes, a challenge thrown down at her worn brogans; then, the narrowing of her eyes and the set of her chin said her temper had kicked a degree higher.

"Well, you've certainly come to the right place. Let me show you our ancestral home." Nathaniel tried to pull open a wooden door and failed. Rafe reached past him to push open the door. He glanced at Demi who hadn't moved, still glaring at him. Rafe smiled slowly, pleasantly. This time, he allowed his teeth to show, because he knew exactly how and when to bite when the occasion called for it. If he had to push to obtain the castle, he would. She clearly was protecting her father, and while he admired that, his grandmother wanted the Valerians in healthier circumstances, with a hefty, compensating bank balance. Mamie had never forgiven herself for devoting herself to building Palladin, Inc. and ignoring Lloyd's needs as a boy.

If Mamie wanted the Valerians to be rid of the castle, their lives and fortunes returned, Rafe would complete her plan. Mamie would want him to be kind—as much as he could be—and to make the Valerians feel as though they were transferring their castle to someone who would care for it. "Nice" took time and Rafe glanced at Demi's knotted laces; the Valerians did not have time, nor did he. It was not a commodity that he wasted.

Systematic and keeping to his schedule, Rafe made a mental note to call Joel from his car phone and tell him he would be late for supper.

He took the camping lantern from Dr. Valerian. The main room was a dark, cold, stone cavern, soaring upward to a chipped molded ceiling. Wind hurled from the huge yawning fireplace and down the winding stone steps as they crossed the stone floor to another door. Nathaniel gestured to the rock slabs, the mortar chipped between them. "My daughter will be raising herbs— chamomile, basil, sweet wood, lavender—and once those are scattered about with rushes, this hall will be grand. We're certain we can duplicate the Montclair tapestry—when she has time to do the needlework. Since the Tallchiefs have added a vermillion stripe to the Fearghus plaid, I'm certain we should do that for our castle...something to blend the English medieval element, with the Native American Tallchief. My daughter is extremely creative and I'm certain she'll come up with something appropriate. Ah, here we are at the library," Dr. Valerian stated proudly, and again Rafe helped him with pushing open the wooden door. Two hinges of the three were unfastened and dangled from one screw, the wood of the door frame rotted.

A tiny black heating stove warmed the shadowy room, a metal pipe ran out the window, secured by duct tape. A wooden shutter banged near the window, threatening to shatter it. Books lined the wooden shelves and were stacked on a long folding picnic table. On the stone wall, a Native American bow hung, crossing an English longbow. A basket held trade beads and an awl, and a Bowie knife sheathed in fringed leather. A Native American trade hatchet hung by thongs; a beaded quiver of arrows hung by a bow.

"That was Liam Tallchief's. He was the son of Una Fearghus and Tallchief, the Sioux chieftain. Liam married Elizabeth Montclair and this was her family's hunting lodge in England. It's quite a romantic story. We have gathered much of Liam and Elizabeth's things including her letters to their son, Jake, and a small velvet bag of crystals that Liam once gave her. Liam and Elizabeth returned here from England, you know. Elizabeth wasn't happy at the time for Liam had kidnapped her and their son. But I think she must have loved him from first sight. Elizabeth was not a woman who allowed herself to be kidnapped or dragged anywhere she did not want to go. The castle is sitting on the very spot of their log home. And just a few miles from here is Tallchief Mountain. Yes, it's all very romantic, more beautiful than a good love sonnet."

Sonnets. Rafe smiled tightly and dropped the word onto the cold floor. He had no illusions about romance, or that it would come to him. Nathaniel's emotional attachment to the land would present problems and raise the price. Rafe inhaled slowly and wondered how Palladin, Inc. could use the castle as a tax writeoff.

Rafe watched Demi pit her weight against the old wooden door, then he reached past her to close it easily. She glared up at him through her glasses; she didn't like help.

Too bad. Mamie wanted to undo the wrong her son had done

the Valerians, and Rafe always succeeded. He smiled at her again. "Palladin, Inc. is prepared to offer a more than fair market value for—"

"Our home? Our dreams? No, thank you, Mr. Palladin, we are quite comfortable here and have no intention of selling." Her voice came clear and crisp, laden with pride.

While Rafe admired her loyalty and pride, he had a job to do. "You might change your mind."

Her smile was too sweet. "I don't think so. Living here is my father's dream. We purchased it years ago before moving completely here, and we're quite happy." She continued to look at him while the shutter banged at the window.

"Improvements cost," Rafe stated logically and found himself enjoying the way the dim light crossed her lips, highlighting the soft curve.

"We're aware of that. However, that isn't your concern, is it?" she asked brightly, and adjusted the shawl around her father's stooped shoulders.

"Still. I'd like to see the rest of the castle—if you have time." Rafe bent and added another piece of wood to the stove, noting that it was no more than a twig. The Valerians needed warmth and comfort, not pride. Rafe's father, a predator, must have enjoyed reaping the Valerians' money, and Rafe had been a part of it. He inhaled again, pushing back emotions that could interfere with business.

Demi looked at her father. "Father, would you mind checking on dinner and setting the table? Here, you take the lantern and I'll light a candle. I'll show Mr. Palladin the rest of the castle. There's nothing like viewing an authentic castle by candlelight."

She ripped open a box of matches and jerked one across the box. Over the tiny flame, her meaningful glance said that she wanted to speak with Rafe alone.

Nathaniel frowned. "I thought he might want to stay overnight and see its glory in the light of day. I thought we could chat after dinner in here, perhaps play chess—you know you have no patience for that, Demi—and I could smoke my pipe and if he's interested in English castles—''

''I am,'' Rafe answered Dr. Valerian's silent plea. Demi obviously ruled the palace and Rafe wanted to see what happened when she was challenged.

Demi inhaled sharply. ''Mr. Palladin has to be going. He's a busy man and we're expecting a blizzard that could last for days. I'm certain that photographs would satisfy his curiosity, and I'll be happy to send them to him. We'll discuss this later, Father, after I've shown him upstairs. Now, please, relax a bit in the kitchen. Or you might lie down in your bedroom. It's nice and warm from the kitchen heat.''

Dr. Valerian shivered and sneezed. ''I might just do so. Our bedrooms are actually the cook's quarters, next to the kitchen, and very comfy.''

Demi glanced at Rafe, asking that he support her suggestion; her father needed warmth, not the drafty, icy rooms upstairs. Nathaniel looked fragile and pale in the lamplight. ''Go on, Father. I can give Mr. Palladin all the information he needs.''

Two

Demi hurried up the stairs, holding the candle high. She was furious with Rafe Palladin for staying, for not taking the hints she'd thrown at him. He'd come out of the February ice, snow and mist as if he were some great black knight, intent upon tearing away her father's castle.

There were clearly no love sonnets in his heart. Cold and ice hovered around Rafe Palladin like a cloak, his expressions seldom changing. The fierce lines on his face were hard, like knife-point edges of Elizabeth Montclair's crystals. Demi paused and turned to him, raising the candlestick to study his face—rugged, tough, day-old stubble darkened a relentless jaw, his green eyes too keen, picking her pride. The man towered over her, exuding wealth. He'd spotted her thrift-shop purchases immediately and knew that he had the advantage of money and its power, the ability to kidnap her father's dreams. Rafe Palladin moved slowly, not a movement wasted, a powerful man, no doubt enhanced by hours at an expensive health spa. Unlike Demi, he seemed to circle every word before it left his well-formed mouth, his gaze taking in information, hoarding it until he needed to use it. He didn't take obvious hints, and *he was challenging her.*

Demi inhaled slowly, preparing her logic, which she used with the males in her life—her ex-husband and her father. It was she who made the decisions for them, dealt with reality as they lived their dreams. Rafe's slow, precise drawl challenged her. Males rarely challenged Demi, not even towering, wealthy ones with spa-molded muscles. She spoke in a hushed, hurried tone, eager to send Rafe on his way. "I sent you a letter. I said we would not sell under any circumstances and that my father badly wanted to keep our heritage."

She whirled away, furious with herself for letting her temper rule her. Shrouded in obvious wealth, reeking of expensive tastes from his flat, thin, gold wristwatch to his Italian shoes, what would he know of loving and heritages?

Rafe was a precise man—alert, intelligent and wanting to tear away her father's dreams. She glanced back at him and found his gaze locked on her hips, probably noting the small tear in her sweater, which she had not repaired. She tugged her sweater down, used to stares condemning the Valerian misfortunes. "Hurry up. I've just started tea and I need to check on Father. Sometimes he begins reading and forgets to draw the covers over him."

Demi loved her father and he loved the land and the castle, therefore, she would protect them. She turned back to Rafe, whispering sharply, "You can't have this castle. Go find your own. This one is taken. I'm certain you can pick one up for a bargain somewhere."

"This one *will* be a bargain if the taxes aren't paid," he murmured in that cool, deep, slow drawl, which echoed off the stone walls.

"You've had experience with that, no doubt." She held the candle up as she made the first turn in the winding stone staircase. "We don't have insurance, so don't fall."

She took another step, and turned to find him looking at her, his eyes on a level with her own. "I will not let you tear apart my father's dreams. Now, we both know that you represent a corporation that is bigger and ultimately more powerful. But I am not entirely defenseless. Newspapers love stories like this—the human interest stories of little people holding on to their heritages, fighting big, strong, heartless corporations. Don't think I won't participate in a fight, Mr. Palladin. I write a rousing letter, unlike your drab business one."

Rafe stared at her—cold, hard, immovable and big enough, powerful enough, to hurt her father. His left eyelid twitched, just once. "It was a business offer, stated in business language, not a sonnet," he asserted in a logical, deep tone that lifted the hair on the back of her neck. "You'll either accept, or you won't."

"Your business letter showed no heart, Mr. Palladin," she shot back. "I could not find an ounce of your love for English history or for castles, or for the land—there are almost fifty acres of woods and game, and fish fill the streams. There are another ten acres of lush fields, perfect for grazing, once they are fenced—which I intend to do."

"Fencing is expensive to have done…and you know how to fence, of course," he drawled, challenging her again.

Faced with frustrating defeat, she turned and hurried around the next curve of the staircase. Rafe followed her slowly, glancing at the airy upstairs quarters, which had been the sleeping rooms. He resembled a black knight prowling through the castle he would lay siege to, his emerald green eyes slashing, searching out its strengths and weaknesses. Demi's anger inched higher. "If you're looking for ancient treasures, we're fresh out. If you're looking for ghosts, they stayed in England."

She hoisted the candle higher and led him down the hallway, motioning with her free hand. "Rooms. Just rooms, no bathrooms. The only bathroom is the one downstairs, added on years ago in this country. The plumbing is horrible. If you leave quickly, I'm certain you can find suitable, warm accommodations elsewhere.''

She watched as Rafe slowly opened a bedroom door and wind from a broken window riffled his neatly clipped hair. He scanned the boards across the windows; Demi held her breath while he noted her first carpentry efforts and the duct tape hanging loosely from the broken glass. If she'd had a power saw instead of a rusty saw and a hammer, she could have done much better. Duct tape usually never failed her. The flickering candle mocked her efforts to block drafts and to care for her father's health.

Rafe scanned the barren room and then went on to open each of the six doors down the hallway, leaving her to follow. ''The rooms are a nice size. Wooden wardrobes would take the place of closets. One room could be converted into a spa and bathroom combination.''

Demi did not want him to state the pluses of her castle. They were scarce enough without sharing them. She pointed to another wooden door. ''Attic. No crazy relatives locked up there. Sorry, not a one. No ghosts rattling chains, either.''

To her annoyance, Rafe took the candlestick from her hand, opened the door and moved silently up the steps to the freezing attic, leaving her to follow him. Demi stiffened automatically; in her experience, men took direction from her. After all, she'd always been capable, devoted and selfless. They could trust her to make the right choices. She'd taken care of her ill mother and her father and merely added her husband to the mix. After her mother had died and Demi divorced Thomas, she went back to taking care of her father. The task was not resented and given in love; though he frequently forgot her, her father loved her just as deeply. She hurried up the stairs after Rafe, noting how much space his body took in the passageway. ''I think you should leave immediately, Mr. Palladin. Your car surely can't withstand the freezing temperatures and if you don't leave now, you could be stuck here *for days*. I'm certain you have other business that must take priority—''

She studied his tall body from his broad shoulders down to his well-polished shoes. To feed a man of his size would destroy the meat reserve she'd carefully measured for her father's health.

In the shadows, he turned to her. "To obtain this castle and to see that you and your father are well compensated is my only concern. If you were to sell, the profit would be hefty and your father could have a nice, comfortable, healthy home. You've lived here since last June and you couldn't pay your taxes. Why don't you make it easy on yourself and on Dr. Valerian?"

Fear skittered along Demi's flesh, chilling her more. Rafe had neatly pinpointed her greatest fear: her father's health. "Are you saying that you are...prepared to set siege to our land?"

"I'm saying you are in a tight spot and your father needs medical attention."

Demi swallowed. Her father's cough had grown worse, despite the expensive medication, and now she noted that his cough had deepened and came more frequently. She wrapped her arms around herself. "He won't leave and this is his dream."

Rafe moved out of the shadows, reminding her of a warrior approaching his intended captive. In the flickering candlelight, he made her ex-husband's attempts at intimidation look childish. Rafe towered over her, expensively dressed; his shoes probably cost more than the taxes owed on the castle. "What are your dreams, Demi? This sale could make everything possible for you."

"I want my father to be happy. He's never been more happy in all the while since my mother died, and to be truthful, before she died. If you left without bothering my father with the details of our financial situation, I would be grateful."

"I can't do that. I can't leave until this is resolved. You could have a business. You ran the student database system at Marksley College. The sale of this property could enable you to enter a business you like and it would provide for your father. I could help you find the right business—"

"I see. You would help me 'acquire' someone else's loved

property, and their dreams, is that right? Exactly how did you know about my former position?'' Rage hurled through Demi; she was a private person and— "My ex-husband contacted you, didn't he? Thomas wants a percentage of this property, doesn't he? But this was purchased prior to our marriage, so it is my father's and *mine*." Thomas had his new wife, he didn't need Demi's father's dreams. Perhaps Esmeralda was not as frigid as Thomas had accused Demi of being; Esmeralda simpered and cooed and was incapable of managing schedules, checkbooks and bills, let alone managing on a skimpy, minor college professor's budget.

While Demi was thinking of Thomas, Rafe placed his hand on the back of her waist and propelled her toward the door. "I always make it my business to investigate the players," he said simply.

"I've never played." Unused to the direction given by a man's touch, Demi walked the first few steps, then stopped abruptly and turned. She looked the long distance up from his gray-and-blue tie to his deep-set green eyes and the humor she found there nettled. "How nice. You probably know how my father cashed in his retirement and sold our small home and how I did the same and how we purchased this property. Your father may have sold us a money pit, but to us, it is a heritage and we intend to stay. You're acting as a mercenary for Palladin, Inc. I don't know what your reward would be, but you are not claiming it in this business coup. I will fight you with every breath in my body, for I love my father, Mr. Palladin, and nothing or no one will shatter his dreams. You will eat with us, because my father has invited you. And then you will pack yourself into your very expensive car and remove your wealthy self from Valerian land."

Hours later, Demi glared at Rafe, who seemed to enjoy the hospitality she resented giving him. Seated at the table, rather his legs sprawled along a good distance of it, and playing chess with her father, the acquisitions chief of Palladin, Inc. had devoured a huge portion of her stew and freshly baked bread.

His manners upset her. They were gallant and old-fashioned as he opened doors for her, pulled out her chair, and there was that odd touch at the back of her waist to guide her.

She'd guided herself, and others, all her life. He'd even lifted the slow-cooker to the table, as though it were too heavy for her— for her, who had done most of the labor on the castle.

Demi studied the sock she was darning, her thoughts locked on the man who had invaded her home. From the looks of him and his expensive car parked in the ramshackle garage next to the Valerians' old pickup, Rafe was slumming and enjoying it.

A woman's castle was her home; she should not have to fend off giants and mercenaries. But if she must, Demi knew that she was qualified to protect what was hers.

His expensive down sleeping bag, neatly rolled and waiting at the door, topped by his leather shaving kit, mocked her plans to tell him that the Valerians barely had bedding enough for themselves. Demi missed a stitch—who would know that the man kept a sleeping bag in his BMW?

With his light gray shadow stripe shirt rolled back to his forearms, his tie tossed over his jacket on a chair and his vest opened for comfort, Rafe Palladin had clearly made himself at home—in her home. He dismissed her obvious hints that he should leave as though shedding gentle spring rain.

Demi did not feel gentle; she felt very, very angry with Rafe Palladin. She glanced at the dark hair escaping the top opened buttons of his shirt and realized that Rafe disturbed her—but then that was only because he represented a threat to her home, not because...not because. Obviously her father was enjoying the chance to play with someone who presented a challenge and did not fidget and groan throughout the game. Rafe played a quick, intuitive game, placing her father in check. She did not like the way Rafe had looked at her and murmured, "Checkmate."

Demi jabbed her darning needle through the sock. "I know

about business games, the ones where the predators lure their prey
into feeling comfortable before they pounce."

She looked up to find Rafe's shielded gaze upon her. He wasn't
happy with her...well, that made them even, because if it were
up to her— Their gazes locked, like clashing, raised swords, and
Demi refused to look away.

"What was that you said about predators and prey, Demi?" he
asked very smoothly in that raw, deep purr that caused the hair
on her nape to rise.

Rafe lay in a second-story bedroom, directly over the kitchen
area. He stretched within the warm confines of Palladin's new
sleeping bag design, and let his thoughts roam. They shot straight
for Demi Tallchief. A very frugal woman, she was not used to
being sheltered, touched or guided into anything. She was bossy,
preferring those people near her to be in their designated places.
She deeply loved her father, her loyalty and devotion painfully
clear. Demi would sacrifice for him, fight for him and never ask
anything for herself. The totally selfless woman...like Belinda,
who had taken a baby who was not hers and protected him.

Should he tell his brothers...his half brothers? Rafe corrected
himself. There had never been secrets between them and whatever
else had happened in his life, he'd always belonged to them. Now,
he didn't.

He placed his arms behind his head and studied the candlelight
flickering on the shadowy stone walls of the room. The sleeping
bag, fashioned for Arctic cold, was warm enough, especially with
the kitchen's heat warming the stones beneath his insulated, thin
mattress. The mattress, a high-tech product of Palladin, Inc. absorbed and kept body heat. His overcoat, adjusted over a boarded
window, provided protection. The room was warmer than those
he had known as a child, or the tents he and his brothers had
camped in on their fly fishing trips in Montana. Rafe smiled
slowly into the night. Demi Tallchief had wanted to make certain

he was uncomfortable; she had offered to give him an authentic experience of sleeping in a castle bedroom.

He listened to the footsteps coming up the stairs, the sounds echoing eerily. The precise, quick step was typical of Demi's movements: hurried, determined and always on a mission. Her hands were always busy—small, slender hands, too fragile to do the work she'd done. The lantern light, which slid beneath his door was blocked in two places by Demi's brogans. She rapped lightly. "Mr. Palladin?"

"Come in." Rafe had been looking forward to her next attempt to pry him from her castle.

Demi entered the room quietly and eased the door closed. The drafts fluttered the hem of her nightgown. The blanket she wore over her nightgown settled around her shoulders and hips. For a moment, the candlelight provided an interesting, shadowy view of long slender legs. She lifted the lantern to find him and the lush shadowy curve of her hip caught him. Demi Tallchief was definitely curvaceous in contrast to his new relatives, the Tallchief women's, long lean lines. Yet that same force of personality, that same determination swirled around her. Rafe turned slightly, catching the scent that was very feminine and uniquely hers.

The womanly curve contrasted her crisp tone, which shot at him like a spear. "I hope you're comfortable, Mr. Palladin."

He noted her tone—confident that she had made her point and made him unwelcome. "Rafe," he reminded her. "I'm quite comfortable."

"Not too cold, I hope?" Her long hair rippled down her shoulders and fell to her waist, gleaming and swaying exotically as she moved.

"Just comfy." His fingers ached to stroke the silky sheen, to wrap his fists in it and— Hell. Rafe frowned. He was feeling delicate and lonely, and a desirable—if hostile—woman had entered his room. In tune with his well-kept body, Rafe recognized certain rising pressures that he had not serviced for years and then only because it seemed a practical release and satisfactory for his partner.

Did Demi—goddess of the harvest—know how dangerous it was to enter a man's room late at night, without her father's protection? Did she know she was missing the middle button of her nightgown? When she placed the lantern on the floor, the shadows revealed a red-hot shade of a lace camisole peeking through the gaping buttons of her nightgown.

Rafe hadn't expected the slam of his desire, his heartbeat kicking higher. The red lace, beneath the worn flannel rosebud sprigged gown, was more effective in stirring him than—Rafe realized it had been years since he'd seen a woman in sexy lingerie. His emotions for his ex-wife, Sara Jane, ran to brotherly protection. Though he had been celibate during their marriage, and had given her son the Palladin name, sex had never been a part of their relationship.

With Demi in the room, every molecule of his body was tuned to her scents, the curve of her lips, her ankles, slender and pale, above the ugly, practical brogans. He swallowed tightly when her breasts rippled softly, the crevice between them deep, as she leaned closer, preparing to make her point. Sexual excitement was definitely the case when this ill-tempered, bossy woman came near him. That grated. Rafe preferred to choose his prospective intimates.

He was just studying her slender, naked ankles above her brogans when a matching shade of red-hot silk dropped to pool at her feet. Every molecule in Rafe's body jolted to alert. His mouth dried and he ordered his heart to start beating again.

"Oh, dear. I was so intent upon talking privately with you that I forgot I was trying on—Demi's De—ah, lingerie. I haven't sewn on the elastic waistband yet," Demi muttered, flushing as she bent to hold the red lace and silk material, preparing to step free. "I've got on shorts, you know. It isn't as if my underpants—"

Her brogans caught. She unbalanced, Rafe reached for her, and she tumbled upon him full-length. For a heartbeat Rafe wallowed in the silky slide and fragrance of her hair, then the rest of his body kicked into overdrive.

Beneath the sleeping bag's down layer, Rafe's body responded to the full curves of her breasts. His hand rested on a flannel-covered hip that was lush and firm and— He forced himself to breathe quietly, reining in the immediate lash of desire, which had startled him.

Oh, well, fine, hell.

Rafe always planned his desire, scheduled his few affairs into his life—quiet, dispensable affairs, easily dismissed without lingering effects. With Demi close to him, he barely restrained himself from fusing his mouth to her soft one.

He wanted to fuse his body to hers, sink into her and— An emotionally cautious man, Rafe's thoughts startled him. He'd never been fascinated by a woman before, and he'd avoided bossy, militant personalities throughout his lifetime.

Demi's hair tumbled around him, a silky strand clung to his day-old stubble, tantalizing him; she smelled like fresh flowers and— His fingers splayed wider on the round, firm curve of her bottom. His other hand settled into a neatly indented waist. *Demi Tallchief was stacked and warm and—*

She blinked at him, her breath hitting his face in short bursts. When she pushed away, Rafe realized he had instinctively held her tighter.

"Are you all right?" he managed to ask, aware of the two firm mounds cushioned on his chest. Little kept him from ripping away the sleeping bag to feel her softness against his chest. He realized he had just shuddered and groaned, his fingers pressing into the lush flare of her hips.

"Mr. Palladin?" she whispered unsteadily. Steam fogged her glasses as she peered down at him. "I hope you're not taking ill. Your color seems to be rising and your nostrils just flared."

He jerked his hand away, too aware of the raging need within him, and disgusted that his desire could be so easily read. "I am sorry."

"I don't see why. You've done nothing wrong. I was merely trying on my lingerie—I'm a seamstress—and suddenly I knew I had to appeal to you on another level."

Rafe knew exactly on what level she appealed to him. He wanted to dive into her warmth, feasting upon her.

She glared at him over her small, round spectacles. "Don't tell me you're comfortable, because you are not. Other than me squashing you, this room is not up to your high standards, I'm sure. In the morning, do not expect crepes and strawberries. I serve oatmeal. It's filling and cheap."

"I've always loved oatmeal."

"You are a difficult man, Mr. Palladin." She clenched her hands and inhaled slowly, evidently preparing to pit herself against him. She straightened her glasses with the tip of one finger. "What would it take for you to remove yourself the very first thing in the morning?"

"You." He reached out to smooth a silky strand of her hair. Demi had no idea of how attractive she appeared, the candlelight smoothing her high Tallchief cheekbones, her gray eyes smoky with emotion, her lips soft and moist and her face framed with all that exotic, fragrant, glossy raven hair.

"Me? What do you mean?" Shocked, Demi blinked down at him.

"You would have to tell me that you can pay your bills and that your father's health is being treated."

As she scrambled away from him, Demi's knee collided with his aroused body. Rafe grunted and grimly stiffened against the pain. She plopped down on the edge of his sleeping bag, staring blankly at him while she straightened her clothing and righted her glasses.

While she was considering an answer, Rafe turned on his side to face her. He gently tugged her brogans off and eased the red lace from her ankles. He eased her bare feet against his hip and covered them with one hand, his thumb smoothing one delicate high arch. Unfamiliar with the gentleness steeping through him,

Rafe concentrated on Demi as she clutched the red lace to her. "You can't have this castle," she whispered desperately. "I won't let you."

"There comes a time to be reasonable and put dreams into perspective," he began, tucking her feet closer to him, warming them with his body and his hand. He wished he could protect her, this woman with heart and dreams, while he had come from a cold life, believing in little but survival.

"We are managing. But Father's medicine and doctor visits are necessary. If the library hadn't needed the dehumidifier and heater to protect Father's books from moisture—" Demi inhaled sharply. "Any home of this size and age would require above-average upkeeping expenses and we all have to live somewhere. But there is romance in this castle, Mr. Palladin—"

"Rafe," he reminded her. "I think all of our negotiations would go easier, if you called me Rafe."

"We are not negotiating." She arched a delicate black brow at him. "You do understand romance?"

That pointed remark hit home. Rafe had never tried to understand gentler emotions, especially romance. "I am thirty-five—" he began in his defense.

"Romance, Mr. Palladin, not crude, unfulfilling sex. There is a difference, and this castle holds the story of a perfect romance. It must be protected from a heartless corporation. I think if you took this idea back to your grandmother, she would understand. You could return to your normal slice and dice business affairs."

"Please explain." Rafe did not believe that sex with Demi would be unfulfilling.

"See? You don't know anything at all about this special castle, the emotional tethers to us. Very well, I'll have to tell you." Demi shivered and glared down at him. "There you lie, big and hard and so very male, absolutely comfortable in all of that and your nice thick sleeping bag. I am not about to tell you a bedtime story—"

"I want to make things right for you and your father, Demi," Rafe stated slowly, meaning it.

Both thin black brows arched instantly. "Charity?"

"Equal terms. I'm very good at working out details, Demi." Rafe stared at the red lace clutched against her chest. His body jerked painfully, just once, and he forced himself to relax. The word, "romance," taunted him.

He reached to his open bag, extracted a thick pair of socks and tossed them to her. "Put these on. Your feet are freezing. I really would like to hear what you have to say, but tomorrow might be a better time. Of course, I'll have to stay then, won't I?"

She glared at him and jammed on the socks. "You know very well that there is a blizzard outside. The radio's weatherman predicts at least another two feet by morning. I'm afraid we're trapped with you for the duration. I just want this settled before you and Father talk in the morning. I don't want you to upset him...Rafe," she added in an apparent bid to soften him. "And then you can spend the rest of the time—play chess with him, let him tell you about Liam Tallchief and Elizabeth, but you must leave as soon as possible."

Rafe was not easily pushed into anything. He could have ended the discussion quickly, but instead, he wanted to keep Demi close. She shivered and on impulse, Rafe tossed a pair of lightweight thermal pants to her lap. "If this discussion is going to last for more than a few minutes, you might put these on."

"I'm quite warm, thank you," Demi said as she shivered and chafed her legs. She frowned at Rafe and added, "Oh. Of course. Thank you. Anything to set you in a pleasant, pliable mood."

Rafe nodded; he doubted that his mood would be pleasant throughout the night.

Demi spared little comfort for herself, moving quickly to shield her father. If she kept up the pace in this gloomy, damp, freezing rock, she'd be ill as well and Mamie would not be happy; Rafe could not have her poor health on his conscience. Rafe inhaled grimly; the Valerians were leaving the castle.

She glanced at his bare shoulders and chest. "I would think you'd be wearing the top of these thermals... Close your eyes, please. I'm not certain about dressing in front of men."

"I prefer no clothing when I sleep." Rafe closed his eyes. Here in this lonely cold night, he would have agreed to anything to keep Demi near him. "You were married."

Clothing rustled and the sleeping bag tightened as Demi pulled on his thermal underwear. Rafe liked the idea of her wearing his clothing, of it keeping her warm. When had Demi cared for her needs, rather than her father's?

"Yes, but...Thomas wasn't...exactly... You are quite different."

"I see." He'd lied. Rafe wanted to tug Demi into his arms and into his sleeping bag, curling around her, protecting her, fitting his hand to her breasts, cradling them. He stiffened, fought another groan and shifted to a more comfortable position.

"You can open your eyes now, Rafe." Clearly Demi was making an effort to use his name to further her cause.

She looked like a young girl, seated on a corner of his sleeping bag, her legs crossed in front of her, his thermal underwear almost covering the socks dangling off the ends of her toes.

She huddled in her blanket. "Now about the castle's romance... You see, Tallchief was a Sioux chieftain who captured Una Fearghus, a bondwoman who was deserted, left to fend for herself near here. Tallchief thought to tame his captive bride and before long, it was a matter of who had captured whom. Their son, Liam, a half blood and one of their five children, grew up near here and life was not easy for the Tallchiefs. Una had to sell her dowry to keep Tallchief land. My cousins are reclaiming it, and each piece has a legend, according to Una's journals. Liam fitted neither race, but he moved easily within both. Then one day, not far from here, he was taken by a gang—cruel men with dark hearts, white men more savage than the Native Americans they hated. After staking poor Liam to the ground, they set about drinking during the day, and Liam knew that he would die that night."

Demi inhaled and rocked herself, looking toward the water-stained ceiling as if stepping into another time. "There he was, staked out and certain for death. Just then, Lady Elizabeth Montclair's hunting party came by, as many royals hunted in the New West, complete with greyhounds and high tea in the afternoon, not the sort of roughing it we usually think of. She and her sister were captured immediately and taken to where Liam was staked on the ground. The criminals wanted to kill her sister, for she would not submit to their lusts—"

Demi leaned down and frowned pointedly at Rafe over her glasses. "Lust, as defined as a cold emotion without the element of romance. We are talking quality emotions here."

"I get the picture." He had a picture of Demi snuggled down beside him in his sleeping bag, pale soft limbs warm against him. He fought a groan.

"Well, then, to continue...Lady Elizabeth tried to save her sister, and the gang was amused by her begging. How badly did she want to save her sister? they asked and offered her a bargain—if she would...make love with Liam—still staked upon the ground, she would save the lives of her sister and herself, and the savages would not—you know...have them. Well. Nothing else would do, though Liam did not want this situation, you understand. There he was, lying helpless, bound and gagged, and furious as Lady Elizabeth agreed, asking for a bit of privacy. Thank goodness they gave her that. They would know the truth of her capture of the savage, they said, by her expression. So, Elizabeth placed herself upon Liam, despite his furious objections, and she quite simply had him—no easy task as she was, you know...an untutored woman. I just don't see how that part was possible, but to continue...the gang knew somehow, it is said, by her rosy, confused expression and Liam's murderous one, that she had succeeded."

Rafe smiled into the shadows. Whatever her husband had shared with Demi, it hadn't been the intimacy of talking about sex. "Lady Elizabeth was no longer a virgin and Liam was not happy that he did not have a choice in sharing his body. Is that about it?''

Demi stared at him blankly. "How can you possibly condense something so beautiful?"

"So then, you think it is acceptable for a woman to take a man, staked to the ground. To press her advantage over someone who is helpless and at a disadvantage."

Demi's head shot up. "I do not like the comparison between Palladin, Inc. capturing this castle and Elizabeth's need to survive. She did what she must to protect her sister and herself. I have no idea of the method she used, but nonetheless, she accomplished her task, because they were free to go. She also made certain that Liam was released. So she protected all three of them."

"And?" Rafe settled down to enjoy Demi's dreamy expression, a restless, fast-moving woman, momentarily captivated by a love story of long ago.

She placed her hand over her heart and sighed. "Biology came into play. Lady Elizabeth became pregnant from that first—intimacy. Liam discovered he had a son living in the Montclair castle in England and he promptly set out to claim his heir. He set seige to the castle—"

She pointed to the window. "He shot an arrow directly into the wooden shutter outside the window, with a note wrapped around it. I believe he used an English longbow. He stated his intentions to claim the woman he considered his wife and his son. Basically he kidnapped her and brought them both back here. By that time, Elizabeth was hopelessly in love with him and he with her. Now *that*, is romance, Rafe, and it is that meeting of hearts that holds this castle safe, as shall I."

Rafe studied the heat in Demi's cheeks, the smoke in her gray eyes. He wanted her for himself, startled with his need to possess and keep Demi safe. "Romance does not pay bills, nor see to your father's health."

"I will do both...Rafe. I will hand launder your thermals and they will be waiting for you in the morning. If we are snowed in, we can call someone to come help you out to the main road. After all, I'm certain you have a full business agenda. You may leave."

Demi was on Rafe's agenda, to stop that fast-talking, pushy mouth with his own. The last person to dismiss him with a snooty, "You may leave," had found that Rafe left when he wanted to go.

She leaned down to study him closely. "You know, that twitch on your left eyelid may need care."

Three

Nathaniel turned to Demi when she entered the library with the afternoon tea tray. Rafe immediately stood and came to close the door behind her, taking the tray. He looked the same as the evening before, towering over her. His dress shirt's sleeves were rolled back at the forearms, a neat thin leather belt circled his waist and there was not even a wrinkle in his suit slacks. She had hoped that he would be so uncomfortable that he would want to leave immediately; instead he looked refreshed.

It was already the middle of February and she had little time to spare on a man who resembled granite, one who would sweep away her father's dreams.

Rafe had almost seemed approachable last night, lying rumpled and warm upon his expensive bedding. She had never seen such broad, tanned shoulders. The light glistening on the hair covering his chest—oh, not too much—just a neat triangular very light mat that was unfortunately stopped by the bedding. His visits to the gyms had paid off, for when Rafe moved, his body fairly rippled, all cords and muscles shifting beneath that wonderful tanned skin—probably due to tanning machines. His big, warm hand, covering her feet, had seemed so safe, she almost thought she could persuade him to leave. This morning, the harsh light found those hard lines on his face, a jaw that compromised nothing and eyes as hard as emeralds beneath his dark brown lashes.

Demi stiffened and smoothed her hands on her apron. She wasn't certain how she felt about Rafe's attention to her as a woman. He was very careful to seat her, to open doors for her. Unused to male attention and help, Demi frowned. Rafe Palladin was an obstacle. A big one with a slow drawl and the ability to stir her temper.

He didn't move quickly from her path as she hurried about her duties, but took just that fraction of a heartbeat to let her know that he moved because it was his choice, not hers. With a lifetime of hurrying to survive, to take care of those she loved and managing men along the way, Rafe's reluctance grated.

This morning, he'd already used a huge amount of wood warming the kitchen and the library. Though the Tallchiefs had supplied a woodpile, Demi had been frugal in using it and had added to it by collecting dried branches from the forest. That precious wood was what had kept her father dry and warm; it couldn't be wasted because of a pampered, wealthy businessman with a slow drawl and who didn't take hints. When Demi had stepped into the tiny shower, it was scented of spice and male. Rafe's zippered leather shaving kit had rested on the shelf with her brush, hairpins, shampoo and powder. Demi had recognized the scent from the sample in her women's magazines. A bottle of the shaving splash cost more than the taxes to keep the castle safe and was designed for "the man in your life. The one you want to lick champagne from your navel and—"

Now, Demi glanced at Rafe as she took her seat next to her father, who was pondering Rafe's knight. The flutter of a napkin onto her lap startled her.

Rafe had placed the napkin on her lap. He smiled down at her, a cool confident smile. The cleft on his chin clearly visible, now that he had shaved. His expression reminded Demi of a wolf, playing at a game he was certain to win.

He stroked one fingertip upward on her nape, an intimate gesture that caused her to shiver and stare at him. Certain that he taunted her, Demi glared at him. The men in her experience wilted when she glared; they usually knew what was expected of them. Rafe's hard mouth curved slightly, mocking her intimidation powers.

He poured tea, obviously comfortable with her father, and sat back to study her. Demi fidgeted; she wasn't used to anyone helping or serving her. Soon Rafe would be on his way and the castle and her father would be hers to tend again. She could begin studying the magazine articles on sensuality again—what women could do to draw men to them, to enhance their love lives with their husbands. She hoped her classes would help those women investing in their sensuality and she could make enough money to— Demi frowned slightly, and eased her brogan away from Rafe's sizable polished shoe, locked to her castle's floor.

Demi listened to the ticktock of the cuckoo clock and thought about all the lovely money she would make, once she convinced her father to visit his sister, Nell, in sunny Arizona.

Nell understood how important it was for her brother to recover. Her notes to him were carefully worded, designed to intrigue him into searching for more English history in a recluse's library.

At precisely four o'clock, Demi's father noted the cuckoo erupting from the walnut clock, and looked up at her. "Teatime already?"

He smiled warmly at Rafe. "I am really enjoying our game. You play very well, an almost creative, yet mathematical precision. My daughter plays with wild abandon as she does everything else."

"Thank you." Rafe's green eyes studied Demi. She noted his big hands comfortably managing the small teacup, as though he could handle everything easily. She doubted he did anything with abandon, rather circling the problem and then streamlining it to suit him.

"She tries," Nathaniel continued. "But my daughter has absolutely no patience for the game, while you are a methodical player, analyzing every move... Oh, by the by, Demi, I've decided to visit your aunt Nell. Rafe has assured me that he will stay here until I return and see that everything is fine here—"

"Father! What are you saying?" Demi was shocked; she had made no arrangements.

Rafe's hard mouth curved slightly. "The snowplow will arrive tomorrow morning and I've arranged transportation for your father."

"Father?" She'd been trying since last summer to have the castle alone and Rafe had accomplished the task overnight.

Nathaniel sipped his tea. "Mmm. Good. Nothing beats a cup of English Gray. You've been trying to get me to visit Nell, to pursue all the information the recluse has hidden. Well, with Rafe here, I feel as though I can leave. I'm certain he'll be much more comfortable in my room than the one he slept in last night. He's agreed to stay, dear daughter. You could come with me and relax a bit with Nell, while I—"

Demi turned slowly to face Rafe. "I'm certain he was just being polite and that given the chance, he would make for...*more comfortable lodging.*" She shot him an expression that said he definitely would not be comfortable in the castle, if she had anything to say about it.

She nudged his gleaming, expensive shoe with her worn brogan, urging Rafe to withdraw his offer. He stared at her coolly; the grim set of his mouth said he wasn't backing down.

Neither was she. "Father, will you excuse us, please? Mr. Palladin, would you please help me in the kitchen?"

She glanced up at Rafe as he opened the door, and waited for her to pass out of the library. Demi glared at him as they crossed the stone floor of the hall, and scowled up at him as he opened the door to the kitchen.

"Exactly what do you think you are doing?" she shot at him, the minute the kitchen door was closed. She opened and closed it again, to prove that she had managed for years without his interference.

"Helping," he answered, studying the top of her head and slowly leaning down to sniff the air above her ear.

She swatted him away, then jabbed his chest with her finger. "I will not have you interfering."

"You're afraid of me, aren't you?" he asked quietly, studying her pale fingertip against his shirt.

The heavy thud of his heart seemed to run from her fingertip right up her arm and Demi jerked her hand away. "No, not at all. I just want you out of my castle."

"I promised your father that I would stay." Rafe leaned against the counter and crossed his arms over his broad chest. "I always keep my promises. My pride demands it."

"Of course, you would stay. That would allow you an insight as how to— You want my castle." Demi fought against launching herself at him, shivering with the effort to find one calm thread within herself, one small bit of logic that would dislodge Rafe Palladin. She needed the castle free of him, so that she could run her operation, make money and keep her father's dream alive.

Rafe looked confident, threatening her plan with just an arrogant tilt of his head, a narrowing of his eyes.

"Sissies won't last here, you know," she volleyed at him in a hushed tone. "It's a hard life—up early in the morning, work all day long and fall into bed at night. There are no comforts, no television, no computers, no gyms, masseuses or tanning salons or anything else to entertain you. You won't last, you know."

"Is that a threat?" he asked in a deep drawl that leaped into her temper and set flame to it.

"Yes!" Demi leaned toward him, her body taut with anger. She ignored the fast drop of his gaze to her heaving chest; she could only hope that he was too ashamed of his behavior to meet her eyes. "You can wait until my father leaves, then you may leave. That way, he'll think you kept your promise to stay for the duration. He will never know that you didn't."

"I would know," Rafe stated logically. His gaze rose slowly to her mouth, and then to her eyes. "What are you up to, Demi?"

"You can't stay," she managed to whisper, before turning and forcing her legs to take her away from Rafe Palladin.

His jerk on her tied apron strings took her back against him. Just an instant, he leaned close to whisper into her ear, "I think I'm going to enjoy this."

Then he released her and strolled out of the door, closing it quietly, like a promise he meant to keep. Demi whipped her loosened apron strings into a fresh bow. "I don't think you will, Mr. Palladin. You will not have the comfort of my father's room and where I putteth duct tape to stop drafts, I can removeth."

"There, my father just called. He is safely at Nell's, and you may be on your way. I won't say a word about you leaving," Demi stated to Rafe after hanging up the telephone. After two days of Rafe interfering with her plans, she had to get rid of him. "I'm certain that you have a family who needs you, a wife, perhaps."

She needed to put all of her energy into preparing for her master plan: The Woman's Sensuality Retreat; she couldn't spare a bit for Rafe. He sat in the kitchen, comfortably sprawled in the old chair and studying his high-tech, tiny, portable computer. An ultraslim telephone rested nearby, ready for Rafe's clipped businesslike tones. They changed when talking to his grandmother, softened, deepened, and became an affectionate drawl.

Dressed in a hand-knit green sweater and worn jeans, Rafe wore expensive, but battered running shoes. He looked like any man, at home in his castle, sipping coffee while he worked. The image nettled Demi.

Two days of avoiding his presence hadn't helped. To avoid

him, Demi had sewn mountains of lingerie, and now with her father safely at Aunt Nell's, she had to dislodge the invader and begin making her moves to make The Women's Sensuality Retreat a reality.

Rafe continued to study the computer screen for a moment, and then clicked it off. He turned slowly to her. "A family who needs me? No, I don't think so. I'm not married. I like it here and I'm not in a hurry to leave."

Demi could feel the conference fees slipping away from her fingers; she gripped the counter until her hands ached. "I couldn't help overhearing. You spoke to a boy, asked him about his mother, and your tone softened. I thought perhaps you might have a family who misses you."

Rafe spoke slowly, as though he had finally resolved a matter that had troubled him. "I'm divorced. The boy is my son, Robbie. I've agreed to let my ex-wife's husband adopt him. She's expecting another baby now and thinks the adoption would be for the best. I agree."

"I see." Demi didn't see. Rafe's voice and expression had said he cared for the boy. How could he give up his son so easily, without a flicker of hesitation?

"Do you?" Something dangerous and challenging flashed in his eyes, quickly shielded by his lashes.

Demi refused to be drawn into a discussion with Rafe. She'd left him to cook and clean for himself, and had not offered him the cozy bedroom near hers. She'd waited for one sneeze, one groan, one sign of his discomfort. He was a pampered businessman, right down to his flat, expensive gold watch. Why couldn't he give her just one little sneeze to pounce upon, proving her point?

Demi shoved the sheer curtains she had purchased from the secondhand store into the washer and wished she could spread and cut the expensive lingerie fabric—the beige and peach—on the kitchen table. The lace from the curtains would be a perfect contrast and make up for the lack of material on her size 20

Midnight Heat model. Over her shoulder, she eyed Rafe's high-tech computer and telephone. "Look. This must be a cost-ineffective waste of your time. I'm certain you'd be much more comfortable in your offices with a fleet of secretaries waiting on your every whim. Don't you miss your secretary? Those nice little things she does for you?"

"Do you always rush everywhere?" he asked, placing his hands behind his neck and stretching the sizable length of his body.

Demi mourned the excess of soap she had just dumped into the washer. She wasn't prepared for the vision of hard muscles leaping beneath his clothing. "I'm on a tight schedule."

She added a tiny bit of fabric softener, saving it for the lingerie cloth she longed to handwash and drape across the main hall to dry. She studied the washer's churning water and tried to remember what Thomas's body looked like, if she had ever felt that leap of excitement when he stretched....

"Schedule?" he asked and instantly the hair on Demi's nape rose. Beneath Rafe's slow drawl lurked the sound of a predator. *Palladin, Inc. would make mountains of money from her idea—*

Demi forced her uncustomary panic into a mental drawer. Her ads would appear in the newspapers by March 1. The Women's Sensuality Retreat enrollment would finance the food and printing costs—and perhaps a plumber could be found to quickly install more bathroom facilities before April 1. It was short notice to enrollees, but last minute advertising had advantages. Spring was the perfect time for women to examine and change their lives, rather like spring housekeeping. If she could just manage to pull off four weekend seminars, she could pay immediate bills and—

If Rafe would just leave, she could cut the fabric and sew to her heart's delight and save the castle. "You had no right to order all that food and fuel to be air-dropped here. I know you needed your favorite blend of coffee, but that helicopter could have easily picked you up and hauled you off. I could have washed your socks for you...you didn't need to order more clothing.''

She capped the fabric softener bottle carefully; Rafe's supplies had been thoughtful, even to the expensive herbal teas, her favorite brand.

"Nick, my brother, likes to think of himself as a rescuer and now and then, we have to let him prove how well he can fly. What if I told you that I liked it here?''

Demi pivoted toward him and blinked. "No one would like it here.''

"Except your father, you and me.''

Demi fought the panic surging up her throat. It was the third week in February; she barely had time to study her clippings, devise seminars on sensuality, sew the lingerie for her gift shop and clean up the castle. She'd managed conferences before, laid out discussions on managing student enrollment databases, which were quite successful. The visitors would have to bring essentials: bedrolls, towels, etc. Nothing could interfere with her plans to support her father's dream. She faced Rafe. "If you think that you're going to run me off in Father's absence, you are mistaken.''

"Oh, well, hell, Demi. Why would I want to do that?'' Rafe asked in a teasing drawl.

Demi blinked at him. She was used to males doing as she asked. No man had ever teased her. Ever. She did not trust the amused gleam in Rafe's green eyes. She refused to be tormented. Demi did not have time to search for Rafe's weak spot and use it, as she had with the other males in her life, manuevering them gently, just where she wanted them—for their own good. "I need you to leave,'' she explained shakily, and hoped he wouldn't press for information.

"Why?''

Darn. She decided to use logic. "You're a businessman. You should understand. You're in my way, Rafe, and I need to use my time wisely, not catering to you.''

"Have I asked you to cater to me? Haven't I followed every one of your many orders, including being in my room exactly at ten o'clock? Didn't I do all my dishes? Haven't I dried down the shower stall—which needs a new head and caulking, by the way? Haven't I turned my cup upside down on the rack after washing it? Haven't I smoothed out the wrinkles in the rug at the kitchen door each time I brought in wood? Haven't I dusted off the snow and rubble from said wood? Haven't I stayed out of your way?"

He had her there. Rafe had cooked his own meals and washed his dishes. He had not said a word when she deliberately ran all the hot water out of the ancient water heater before his morning shower...or when she started washing clothing during his next shower, setting the water temperature to Hot. All she'd gotten for her trouble was a quick, dark look that said he knew the cold-water culprit.

While she was searching for ways he was underfoot, Rafe said, "I hear your sewing machine at night. Did you get the elastic in those red panties?"

Demi fought the quick surge of heat to her cheeks. Perking up her inventory had called for making several pairs in different sizes of her lingerie. She could almost hear the cash register clanging. The snazzy labels, Demi's Delites, would arrive any day. "They weren't panties, they were dance pants, and yes, thank you, I did finish them."

She hurried onto other steps to dislodge Rafe. "You can't just stay here and not work, Rafe. This is no fancy spa, you know. Paying your way would be too easy. I demand that you work for your keep," she finished stoutly, certain that demand would run him off.

Rafe Palladin's presence could threaten the Women's Sensuality Retreat, and destroy her attempt to salvage the castle for her father.

"Okay," he agreed lightly. "Now tell me why you want me out of here so badly."

Demi clamped her lips closed; she couldn't expose her plan to a man who would tear away the castle from her father. Palladin's chief of acquisitions and product development would immediately see the value of the castle as a retreat and vacation site. Palladin, Inc. would make the money she desperately needed.

Rafe stood slowly, rolling his shoulders to stretch his muscles. Demi took a step backward, startled once more by his size. She flopped her best attack at his well-shod feet. "You just remember about working for your keep."

"Okay," he said again, and began punching buttons on his portable telephone. "Nick? I need lumber, carpentry supplies and small power tools. See to it, will you? Plumbing supplies, plenty of caulking, maybe a small jackhammer and a good mortar for stones. The roofing will hold until summer. And tell Joel and Fiona that I'm sorry I won't see them for a while. What's that? Ian turned over on his stomach? The kid is a genius. That's great. Yes, of course, please tell the Tallchiefs that I'm looking forward to seeing them when the roads open. Demi will enjoy the company." Rafe smiled slowly. "She's nasty, thinks life comes from a book, bossy and as close to a drill sergeant as you can get. Other than that, she looks like a compact Tallchief."

As he spoke over the telephone, Rafe's gaze slowly slid over her. "Come prepared to work."

Tallchiefs? Fiona? Demi recognized the unusual name. She stood absolutely still as Rafe looked at her. She gripped the kitchen counter and a tile came free in her hand. She looked at it, the symbol of crumbling plans.

Rafe clicked off the telephone. "I see your mind clicking, Demi, trying to place my relationship with the Tallchiefs. I'll save you the trouble—Joel Palladin is my brother. He's married to Fiona Tallchief, of the Tallchiefs of Amen Flats. Basically, Demi, you and I are related. Now, it wouldn't be very hospitable for you to kick me out of here, would it?"

He walked to her and with each step, Demi felt her plans sinking into the moat. Rafe took the tile from her hand, neatly replaced it on the counter and slowly retrieved a scrap of paper from his jeans' pocket. "You may want this."

Demi stared down at the clipping he had just handed her. The women's magazine article, "Midnight Calls," had nothing to do with the telephone, rather developed a method of a woman seducing a male. The article must have fallen from Demi's well-stuffed portfolio of sensuality articles, which were her only link to a woman's sensuality and desirability. Demi had no personal basis upon which to base her lectures. In her experience with Thomas, plain old sex, was exactly that—plain, fast and unfulfilling.

Rafe slowly removed her glasses and Demi refocused up at him as he asked, "Now, Demi, let's make this easy, shall we? Why don't you tell me what you're up to?"

He leaned closer, blocking out the rest of the room and suddenly Demi realized that she couldn't breathe. "You're taking all my air. Remove yourself," she whispered unevenly, edging back from him.

Though he didn't move, she sensed that Rafe had stiffened, that she had issued some challenge that he couldn't ignore. His gaze darkened as it touched her lips.

She stared at his mouth.

The air between them sizzled; her heartbeat surged to a race she didn't understand.

"Tell me what you know about sensuality," Rafe invited, in a low uneven drawl that skittered along her skin and heated it.

"I'm learning," she whispered shakily, and had no idea why she wanted to fling herself upon him.

His hands rested on the counter beside her, both thumbs stroking her hips. He studied the line of her cheeks, then her ear and down her neck. He studied the heavy sweater covering her bosom. His breathing seemed to quicken. "Just what don't you know?"

Demi leaned back. She'd never felt delicate or feminine, and now Rafe was making her feel— *Feel*. What? Frightened? Wary? Hungry?

She studied him. At close range, Rafe seemed harder, bigger, more threatening. She wanted to soothe whatever tormented him, whatever she had sensed he wore like a shroud of pain. She knew how to soothe males, how to manage them and direct their lives. That is what she would do—manage Rafe Palladin, manage to pry him from her castle and her plans.

He smiled softly. "You scowl when you're planning, Demi. Your expressions are giveaways."

"Please don't stay," she whispered, surprising herself. "You'll ruin everything."

Then Rafe leaned close, placed his cheek against hers and nuzzled it, thoroughly shocking her. "I'm here to stay, sweetheart," he whispered.

She jerked back, stunned. "Sweetheart" did not apply to her, but had been mentioned in the article. Rafe was merely citing what he had read and it did not concern her personally. "Endearments. Yes. I forgot the section concerning those. Good. Thank you."

He frowned slightly, and she stared at the cleft in his chin, fascinated by it. When she looked slowly upward, his left eyelid had just twitched.

Demi parted her fingers, which covered her face, peered through them and hoped that what she had seen wasn't happening.

At seven o'clock in the morning, there were three of them, all towering, green-eyed, dark brown wavy hair, matching clefts in their chins. All happily destroying her plans and her castle with power saws and jackhammers.

For three days, she had worked in her room, avoiding Rafe. There was no avoiding the massive helicopter, hovering and lowering tarp-covered mountains of supplies, or the sound of a power saw ripping through the March 1st air as Rafe repaired the drawbridge. His temporary sealing of the huge fireplace in the main hall had helped to ease the castle's drafts, though she disliked admitting it.

She inhaled shakily and forced her hands into her apron pockets. She'd overslept, troubled by the nightmare of the hovering sound of the helicopter. She'd awakened to the reality of ripping saws, the rumble of men's voices on the second floor. She had dressed quickly in her usual thick sweater, long warm woolen skirt, hose and brogans. She hadn't taken time to braid her hair, but had hurried toward the sounds of hammers and men's voices. She'd had to sidestep the new crate containing a shower stall and the toilet resting outside the bathroom; she'd eased around a mound of boards and crates. The kitchen was filled from top to bottom with grocery sacks, waiting to be unpacked. The main hall was filled with more crates and more boards. One glance outside told her that the hovering sound of the helicopter had not been a nightmare, but a reality.

Dressed in matching coveralls, the three men were busy installing new windows on the second story. One was bent near a huge power saw, trimming narrow boards with an artistic flair; another was holding a window in place while the other secured it. While Demi stood, her brogans locked to the castle stones, the three men stopped working and turned to her.

"You look just alike," she whispered when she could speak.

"I'm prettier," the one by the power saw said, removing his safety glasses. His eyes were the same shade as Rafe's. "I'm Joel."

"Nick," the one by the window said, easing it into place. He dusted his hands, and green eyes the exact emerald shade as Rafe's looked at the man next to him. "That must be her."

"The one and only." The man had to be Rafe; she instantly recognized his slow, deep drawl. "Demi Tallchief. These are my—"

"I know...your brothers." Demi fought to recover. Good Lord, now there were three of them! She tried to rally again. "Gentlemen, I'm certain you have things of more importance to occupy your time. Whatever Rafe has told you, I'm certain he's—"

"Not a clue, huh?" Nick asked Rafe quietly, who didn't answer. He stood, workman's boots braced apart, his hands on his hips, looking just like his brothers, except for the hardness lodged on his face and that twitch in his left eyelid.

Demi trembled, faced with three immovable Palladins. She rarely felt helpless; she always had Plan B, if Plan A failed, but now... There were towering men everywhere, all with clefts in their chins and none of them looking as though they could be budged. Desperation welled out of her. "You can't stay here, none of you. All duplicates must go."

Joel smoothed the board in his hand. "My wife is looking forward to visiting next week. She and the Tallchief women want to come up here and help, too. She'll be really disappointed if we don't have the place nice and warm and the bathrooms working. Fiona and I could sleep in that cozy little bedroom with the fireplace," he said wistfully. "With a five-month-old baby and my son, Cody, around—a little privacy wouldn't hurt."

"He's dying for a second honeymoon. We don't have much time," Nick added. "Fiona is really planning on this. Elspeth, Sybil and Talia are leaving their husbands in charge for one week, while they help. I wouldn't want to tell them that they can't come."

Demi pleaded silently with Rafe, whose expression only hardened.

"We could cancel everything, I suppose. But I wouldn't want to be the one to tell Fiona," Joel offered slowly. "Then there's Elspeth, who agrees that this castle is part of the Tallchief heritage, and she's certain there is a legend hidden here. When the Tallchief women set their hearts to something, I've found that it's a matter of standing back or doing what they want."

Demi heard herself groan. There was no way she could refuse her cousins entry into the castle; they'd welcomed her so warmly into their lives and they shared the same heritage. Meanwhile, her schedule crumbled at her brogans; the castle would fall into the hands of bill collectors—or Palladin, Inc. She fought the tears welling in her eyes, fought the sob churning up her throat, and managed to step outside the door before she gave into crying. She hurried down the steps, sidestepping the various stacked boxes, and ran through the kitchen to the safety of her bedroom.

"Demi?" Rafe's deep voice curled through the last of her sobs. After a half hour, she was down to the sniffing stage. Her first outraged wails had probably shocked the men on the floor above her.

"Go away," she managed to say, curling deeper into her bed, hugging her pillow tighter. She drew the quilt over her head.

Behind her, the bed creaked and sank slowly. "What are you doing?"

"Taking off my boots," Rafe answered in a logical tone as he lay down at her back, taking her into his arms.

She squirmed uneasily. No one had cuddled her since she was a child. Rafe tucked her close against him, spooning his larger body to the back of hers. If she hadn't needed a warm port in her emotional storm, she would have tossed him aside. She resented not having that huggable cat or dog her father was allergic to, and at the moment with his arms safely around her, Rafe provided two hundred pounds of comfort.

"Now is no time for family affection," she said after a sniff. If she escaped him, she'd only run into his duplicates.

"No, you're right. Brotherly isn't on my list," he murmured, drawing the quilt down. His cheek rested against hers, nudging a strand of her hair away to kiss her damp skin.

Defeated, weary, burdened beyond her capacity, Demi gave way to the secure feeling of resting in his arms. "This won't do," she whispered.

"Mmm. What?" His tone sounded distracted, his lips smooth and warm against her cheek.

"Evidently you've been elected peacemaker, and you can't be that, because you instigated the whole invasion. You're guilty, Rafe, don't deny it. You saw that you couldn't have your way alone, so you called in your duplicates with their ties to the Tallchief family. That was unfair fighting. I would have preferred to keep it on a personal level—just you and me. I must have represented a threat to your plan to get the castle, because you called in reinforcements.''

His socked feet moved to push her brogans free. They clunked to the floor, and his feet toyed and warmed hers. His hand reached to claim hers and bring it lightly to his mouth. Demi snatched it back. ''You cannot have your way with my castle, Rafe. I can play just as dirty.''

His lips prowled around her ear and Demi fought to breathe, her pulse racing. ''Now, I know you're trying to console me—''

Rafe turned her slowly, and began kissing her damp lashes. The featherlight kisses eased down her cheeks and to her mouth. She gripped his arm, sinking her fingers into the hard, safe warmth of him. ''Do you know—'' she paused for another light kiss ''—how hard I've worked to keep to my schedule?''

''Mmm. What schedule?''

Under a siege of light, tasting kisses, she fought revealing her soul to him, how warm and safe he felt, how her plans had to succeed. Just once she needed an anchor to depend upon and now Rafe was at hand—she turned to him fully, watched his eyes darken as his arms immediately drew her closer, his hands opening upon her body. He held her as though he knew exactly how to take care of her.

Demi blinked at him through her glasses, which he removed gently. ''I really want you to go,'' she whispered. ''You are interfering with—never mind.''

He drew her very close to him, his body hard against her softer one.

She trembled, aware that the temperature in the room had risen several degrees since he had begun to hold her.

Perhaps it was on this quiet, intimate level that she could make her logic clear to him. She had often found that meeting of the minds could take place anywhere—if both parties were receptive. She studied Rafe's expression—slumberous, waiting, definitely warm...and then there was that slight, unmistakable, yet unreasonable hunger. "I want to take care of you, sweetheart," he whispered unevenly.

"I've always taken care of myself. But on to the matter at hand—"

She inhaled and blinked. Rafe's large hand had just fitted over her bottom, smoothing it. It roamed to her hip, his fingers sinking in slightly as if claiming her. His other hand cradled her head, drawing her cheek to his chest; his chin gently nuzzled the top of her head. He rocked her in his arms, the bed creaking softly beneath them. Demi blinked again and listened to the steady, heavy rhythm of his heart. "You don't understand," she whispered against his chest and stopped as she caught the male fragrance lying beneath the lumber, soap and wood-smoke scents.

His fingers stroked the back of her head, the gentle rhythm a seduction. She let herself drift momentarily, stunned that she had let the matter get out of control; Demi always had everything under control. "You'll be sorry," she threatened weakly.

"I don't think so," he returned firmly, his lips lowering to hers.

Four

"**M**en everywhere. Giants invading my castle," Demi muttered as she glared at Rafe. She swished her broom at him. "Rafe, don't you dare touch another—"

He reached to lift her out of the way as Joel and Nick carried lumber up the stairs. Demi straightened her glasses with the tip of her finger and glared at him. "I know what you're after, and you're not getting it," she snapped and hurried away from him, down to her bedroom.

"We'll see," Rafe said grimly, enjoying the sway of her skirt and the way her sweater shifted on her hips as she hurried. Demi had no idea of how much she excited him, and he wasn't happy about that, either. She made him feel as if his appeal rated right down there with scrubbing floors. She kissed like a child. Demi felt like—Rafe stifled his frustrated groan. There was that Demeter, goddess of the harvest factor and he was definitely in a mood to harvest.

He tramped up the stairs to help his brothers. There was no

reason Demi should excite him. She glared at him, snapped at him. She was bossy, infuriating, uptight and walking into her bedroom had stunned him. Sexy, colorful lacy lingerie had been draped everywhere. It lined the walls, the top of her single bed.

Rafe scowled at Joel's wide grin and dropped back into thoughts about Demi's bedroom, the fiesta of colorful, sexy lace that had greeted him. Demi's bed was too small and cramped and he wanted to peel away that ugly sweater and skirt to reveal all that fine, lush, heated, curved, sweet woman beneath. One look at her today, and he wondered exactly what was sliding against her skin, what mouth-drying symphony of male-devastating lace and color she wore beneath her long woolen skirt and shapeless sweater. Somehow the disguise of all that sweet curved flesh sliding beneath silky lace and hidden by Demi's sexless clothing was erotic, fascinating and criminally destroying to the male mind.

He put too much strength into flinging a length of board aside. Joel and Nick looked at him sharply and Rafe glared back. Well, hell. There was Madeline, of course. He could visit her and stay for breakfast. Madeline Bower was bright, sexy, intelligent and made a man feel welcome. And, she knew how to let go. Hell, he could do with a little petting, with a little tenderness.

When he held Demi, kissed her, everything felt right. As an acquisitions director, and after a lifetime of hard knocks, Rafe knew that "right" feeling meant to hold tight, and he intended to hold Demi very tightly, intimately. He glared at Nick. "Don't get any ideas about Demi," he heard himself snarl.

Nick held up his hands, a female-hunting male yielding the field.

"I think this is it," Joel announced happily and began whistling.

Rafe didn't like the way his brother said, "it." "Hey, I'm in control of my life," he shot back over the sound of a saw ripping at boards.

"You were," Joel, a married man very much in love with his wife, said in the voice of experience.

* * *

Demi held her hands tightly together, aware that Rafe had draped his arm loosely around her shoulders as the Tallchief women approached on snowmobiles.

"I'm perfectly warm," she said after shivering. "You don't need to put your arm around me...I can't possibly pay you for this," she whispered to Rafe. After a week of the huge males tromping around her castle and devouring the tons of food they had cooked, Demi was certain that their female counterparts would manage the final collapse of her plans. She wasn't used to sharing her life, or having it taken away from her. She was desperate. Her ads were in the city newspapers and she could be getting calls at any minute. "Rafe, please make them go home. Do it in a nice way, though, would you?"

He shook her gently. "I can't do that. They're looking forward to this. Now, why don't you tell me your plans?"

Before the snowmobiles came close to the moat, Joel was moving past Demi and Rafe as though nothing would stop him. The moment Fiona's snowmobile stopped, he whisked her out of the seat, drew away her mask and kissed her as if he were starved for her. She flung her arms around him and they went tumbling into the snow. In the next instant, Joel picked her up and ran, carrying his wife into the deep woods.

"Heat wave," Nick noted dryly as the other women paid no attention, unpacking their gear and hurrying to the castle.

"It's not what you might expect," Demi began as the women, Elspeth, Sybil, Lacey and Talia stood in the center of the main hall. Elspeth, Sybil and Talia towered over her, matching the two tall men. Lacey, a petite woman with a mass of curly black hair, somehow complemented the towering Tallchiefs.

"Oh, yes," Elspeth exclaimed with delight, her gleaming black hair matching Demi's, as she took in the main hall. "I can feel a legend in here somewhere, waiting to be cherished. It will turn up."

Sybil's dark red hair lit beneath the new lighting fixtures the Palladins had installed. "Beautiful. I'd love to help find authentic pieces—or you might want to find more of the Tallchiefs' things.''

Talia's blond hair shimmered, a perfect foil to the other tall women, as she walked around the room, her Hessian boots striking eerily on the stone floor. "Man, oh man. Wait until Alek sees this. My husband is an editor for Amen Flats' newspaper and he'll want this story.''

"Dynamite!" Lacey exclaimed. "There's nothing like restoring good solid structure. This should be more fun than my bordello.''

"She and her husband, Birk Tallchief, have a construction business," Elspeth exclaimed coolly as she studied the huge fireplace, currently blocked to prevent drafts. "I can just see mounds of mistletoe and pine boughs across that.''

"The castle cries for good solid, hand-hewn pioneer furniture," Sybil murmured, sweeping out her hand. "A long table there, in front of the fireplace, lined with chairs.''

"It's not much," Demi persisted, hoping that they would soon want the comforts of their own homes. She noted that Rafe stood very close to her and she eased away. Filled with emotion, invaded by her relatives who she could not politely remove, facing an endangered schedule to save the castle, Demi felt her bottom lip tremble. "I...''

Rafe looked down at her sharply. "She's going to cry.''

With a shielded look of terror, Nick seemed to melt into the shadows and the women crowded around Demi, hugging and patting her and comforting her. She glared at Rafe, the invader and despoiler of her schedules and her life. He glared back.

That night, Sybil and Elspeth would sleep in Dr. Valerian's bed. Talia and Lacey would share Demi's single bed, while she made a pallet on the floor. Fiona and Joel slept in a separate bedroom upstairs, the miniature fireplace warming the room. Nick and Rafe used another room. She presented the women with a set of her Demi's Delites lingerie and melted under their glowing praises. "You should market these," Lacey exclaimed delightedly.

"I'll think about it. Thank you." Excitement raced through Demi; she couldn't wait to start sewing again. Demi's Delites were certain to be a success, if gauged by the women's reactions.

With the candles flickering in the bedroom's drafts, the women settled down to talk quietly. "I'm glad you could come," Demi said, meaning it. "Though you really didn't need to work so hard. My goodness, you've almost scrubbed the whole upstairs and Lacey, I had no idea you were such a good carpenter. The kitchen cabinets were so warped they were always coming open."

"Hey. I'm a carpenter and know a good working crew when I see it. Those Palladins are used to working as a team and I didn't want to unravel them. The kitchen seems safe. I'll start power sanding and varnishing tomorrow. You may want to start a slow-cooker for dinner in another part of the house. Or we could use that fireplace in the hall."

"When Joel, Nick and Rafe get the upstairs bathroom done and the hot tub going, I am really going to enjoy it. The view is beautiful—looks straight out at the mountains," Sybil said with a yawn. She stretched elegantly. "Poor Duncan. I wonder what my teenage daughter, Emily, is doing now. He doesn't want her to date until she's thirty."

"You shouldn't have left your families—"

"What? And not give our husbands a chance to appreciate us?" Elspeth's tone held amusement. "Good luck to Emily. Fiona and I had a hard time escaping our older brothers when we were thinking about dating. They intimidated all the boys."

"My father and I can't afford these improvements," Demi began desperately, anxious to make them understand. "Rafe does not seem to be receptive to hints."

"It's a matter of pride—Palladin pride, Demi," Elspeth said softly. "Joel, Nick and Rafe need to do this. Let them."

"Palladin pride?"

Fiona frowned, her expression thoughtful. "Their father left them nothing. They've worked so hard to build themselves into men with pride. I wouldn't do anything that would diminish that—they have their honor. They had a horrible childhood and finally when their father was sent to jail, their grandmother saw how badly they had been treated. She jerked them from the streets, pushed and shoved and molded them into reluctant but good students, and forced them to meet any problems they created—unlike how she had treated her son, Lloyd. Apparently she was too busy with her business to pay attention to him and had covered up his many problems, bought him off, and she was determined not to make the same mistake with her three grandsons. Those early years of tough love paid off and they are dedicated to her, loving her just as she does them. Mamie will never forgive herself for letting her son dupe her into thinking the boys were well tended.''

"I was probably eight years old when I first met Lloyd Palladin and negotiations began for the castle. He seemed to be...unsavory.'' Demi decided not to say anything about Rafe trying to wrest her castle away. She wanted to go to him and hug him and tell him that he was not obligated to take care of her, to stay, working too hard to compensate for his father's sale of the castle. She tried to sleep, calculating how much lingerie she would have to sew and sell to repay everyone. She thought of how Fiona looked at Joel, that steamy soft look and Joel's answering hungry look.

Now *that* was confusing. Rafe's expression, when he looked at Demi, was much the same.

Fiona and Joel and the other Tallchief women were obviously in love. The word terrified Demi; in the name of love, she had given so much, given herself totally to Thomas and became his servant. Yet the Tallchief women did not seem tamed and tethered by love, rather they seemed to thrive as independent women. They had their own interests and needs, apart from those of their husbands.

Demi and Thomas's sharing had involved Demi's serving Thomas.

Demi knew she hadn't been in love with Thomas; she'd simply made a practical, logical marriage to a man she understood. Buried somewhere along the way were her teenage dreams of love and sonnets.

Unable to sleep, tormented by what Fiona had said of the Palladins' childhood and by the romantic love that had escaped her grasp, Demi eased from her bedroom and wandered into the great hall. Rafe stood in front of the blazing fire, one boot braced on the low hearth, his hand against the stone wall as he studied the flames. The light played across his bare shoulders and skimmed the beautiful, powerful lines of his arms and down his long legs.

When he turned his head to her, she saw a darkness that terrified her, a horrible, chilling loneliness. He turned and faced her fully, his hands at his sides, his feet braced wide apart as though to take a blow.

"Come here." His order was quiet and raw, echoing against the stone walls, curling around her heart and drawing her to him.

Rafe didn't want to need anyone. He wasn't a part of this family now, not since he'd read Belinda's letter. He felt as if the anchors he'd known all his life had been torn away and he was sinking into a cold pit. Belinda may have left other letters to her sons; he had to tell Joel and Nick. They had always had honesty between them, unlike Lloyd's dark secrets.

Rafe listened to the fire crackle behind him and watched Demi slowly cross the shadows to him. In her well-washed flannel nightgown and her hair gleaming, falling loosely around her shoulders, she seemed more child than woman. Her gray eyes were huge and rounded in her pale face, her lashes creating feathery shadows on her cheeks, as she reached to place her hand along his cheek, cradling it.

Her softness was his undoing—a thread to someone clean and soft and caring. More than that, he needed Demi as another part of him. He could no more have stopped himself from reaching for her than he could have stopped the sun from rising. Rafe swept her into his arms, felt the soft collide of her body with his and settled his chin over her head. His urgent plea had shocked him; Rafe had never asked for comfort since his childhood. He had learned not to ask, nor expect softness. "Stay here."

"I will." Demi's quiet tone, her cheek against his chest settled the pain that had been stalking Rafe.

Her arms came slowly around his waist. They fluttered for a moment at his belt, then lightly settled on it. She stood stiffly against him, unfamiliar with a man's embrace, yet enclosing him in a soft embrace, which he needed desperately. Rafe threaded his fingers through her hair, smoothing the fine hair at her temple with his thumb. He trembled slightly, suddenly aware of how much he needed her, how much the dark shadows inside him could frighten her.

Demi stirred, raising her hands to cradle his cheeks. "Shh," she whispered. "Don't worry so."

Oh, well, hell, Rafe thought as he fell into her soft, caring gaze. Demi had no idea of the storms ruling Rafe, yet she reached out to comfort him. He could hurt her easily, his rein on his control slipping. Fear seized Rafe; he was as powerful as Lloyd. He could hurt her.

She stood within his arms, her clear untroubled eyes trusting him. He didn't deserve— Her thumbs smoothed the skin near his mouth and she whispered firmly, "Whatever troubles you, Rafe, you will handle perfectly."

"How do you know?"

"Because you're you." Demi stood on tiptoe and kissed his lips, the butterfly-light touch stunning Rafe.

He blinked, staring down at her. She terrified him. Or was it the knowledge that he could be like his father? Ruthless, powerful, abusive...

Rafe didn't like feeling fragile. He didn't like feeling as if he were an uncertain boy in the arms of the woman he desired; nor did he want the woman he desired acting as if she were his mother kissing his bruises.

He realized sharply that he had desired few women and that was years ago, when he was stepping into manhood, testing himself.

"Stop scowling," Demi ordered lightly, and ran her finger between his eyebrows. "You're not frightening me."

"I'm bigger and stronger than you," he reminded her, feeling the shreds of his torment give way to his pleasurable fascination with this woman.

"You're a gentleman. I trust you in this matter." Her proper, polite tone nettled, dismissing him as a man who desired her.

"Am I?" The challenge was too much and Rafe gave into the need to shock her. He cradled her head and took her mouth, unleashing his hunger for her.

"You missed that spot to your left," Demi pointed out to Rafe, who stood on a scaffolding platform close to the main hall's ceiling. The brothers had constructed a sturdy board scaffolding from the floor to ceiling, and while Nick and Joel worked on arched windows and doors, Rafe—considered the more artistic of the three—studiously rebuilt the chipped ceiling plaster.

"A little more to the left," Demi said, trying to help him. Rafe, holding a plaster trowel, glared down at her, looking little like the very warm man who had whispered that she might open her lips to his kiss. She licked her lips experimentally and remembered the interesting flick of his tongue, as though he were tasting her. She almost believed in that moment that a Tallchief legend lurked in the castle and had curled itself around her.

She clutched her notebook, filled with all the notes she was developing for her seminar booklets. All she had to do was to type it up, send it to the printers who were waiting, and—

Demi caught a movement out of the corner of her eye and turned quickly, focusing on the neat pat Fiona had bestowed upon her husband's backside. The leer Joel shot his wife over his shoulder sizzled and promised. Demi hurried to jot down "Backside Pats" in her notebook, then refocused on the male backside above her.

Rafe's backside, when viewed from the floor, was appropriately taut and beautiful, flowing into long, widely braced legs. Demi had never considered herself a connoisseur of male backsides and she had shocked herself. "Oh, Rafe. You need to add more plaster to the design on your right. Two squares over. That little corner there."

Whatever disturbed Rafe Palladin had flown into the shadows last night, but Demi sensed it would return. Meanwhile, Rafe was determinedly, hand over hand, cords and muscles straining in his arms, his legs braced wide upon the board, lowering the platform. Demi was fascinated by the symphony, the beauty of his body.

When the platform was firmly on the floor, he grimly secured it and stepped easily over the rope railing. He placed his hands on his waist. Plaster dotted his hair and shoulders and—Demi refocused her gaze on his bare chest, the white plaster specks a contrast to the dark skin and light matting of black hair. There was so much of him. He grimly stuffed her into his shirt, which was lying discarded nearby.

"This is Italian, very costly and no doubt tailored just for you," she noted, uneasy with the way he had handled her like a child.

"Come on," he snapped and lifted her into the platform, plopping her to her bottom. "Sit there. I don't want you getting a sore throat from yelling up at me every two minutes."

"I do not yell." Demi barely had time to straighten her glasses before Rafe was methodically hauling them upward on the platform.

"Take it easy," Joel warned, his expression concerned.

"I intend to take it very easy," Rafe returned easily.

When he had secured the ropes to the board platform, he crouched beside Demi who was gripping the boards with both hands. His smile was lethal and cold, a showing of his teeth without amusement in his jade eyes. "You've been hovering down there for a good hour, pointing out my mistakes. You'll have a better view this way.''

''What does Joel want you to take easy?'' Demi asked, nettled that Rafe had captured her, when she was usually in control. She peered the distance down to the floor and found Joel and Nick standing, hands on hips, legs braced, scowling up at her.

After a dark look down at her, Rafe stood, picked up the mortar and trowel and began working, ignoring her.

''I don't see what you're so angry about,'' Demi managed unsteadily several minutes later.

Rafe kept on working, slathering plaster into the chipped molded designs, and fashioning the design with his fingers or a big spoon. ''I like sleep,'' he stated darkly as if the short answer would give her all the answers she needed.

Inspired, Demi reached for her notebook. She jotted down, ''Males need sleep for good moods,'' which she would research and expand later.

A glob of plaster dropped to the shirt she was wearing. Rafe's dark look cut to her, found the glob on her breast; he closed his eyes and groaned.

''It's not my fault that you can't sleep, or that your shirt will be ruined,'' Demi shot at him, not understanding why his stark hungry stare would cause her skin to tingle and her breasts to ache and harden.

Rafe returned to plastering and muttered something dark and ominous.

Demi sat up straighter; men in her keep rarely rebelled. ''What? I demand to know what you just said.''

His grim silence infuriated her, she who had always understood and comforted males, she who had taken care of them. ''I would really prefer to be on the floor, if you don't mind. Please,'' she added, aware of her weakness of heights.

His look down at her was not kind. He actually smirked as if he had intimidated her. ''Scared?''

''Not a bit. I was wondering if the soup needed stirring.''

Demi had never experienced the need for revenge, but it began simmering in her now. Payback was on its way to Rafe...just as soon as she thought of something.

He leaned over the rope railing and yelled, "Nick. Stir the soup. We're in conference up here."

Demi straightened. The men in her experience were quiet and maneuverable; they did not shovel orders as if they were used to giving them. Rafe closed his eyes instantly when she noted another spot he had missed. She peered down at Fiona and Joel, wrapped up in a heated kiss at the door of the library. Joel scooped Fiona up, his hands supporting her bottom, her legs curled around his waist and the kiss intensified.

"Rafe?" she asked quietly, curiosity replacing her need for revenge.

"Mmm?" He continued to smooth a rounded design with the back of a spoon, easing it into the old design perfectly.

She noted the distracted male tone her father often used and the safe time to ask questions, which ordinarily might shock him. "Exactly how would an untutored woman like Elizabeth get Liam to respond—you know, harden enough for her to complete the job? I mean, if she is the one on top, actually mounting him, how would she—?"

Rafe was staring at her blankly and Demi felt the slow, hot flush move up from her throat. "Well, I don't understand the mechanics of the Vice Versa," she snapped.

"'The Vice Versa,'" he repeated slowly as if finally understanding her meaning. Rafe's gaze dragged to where Joel and Fiona were kissing each other. "Take that into the library. And shut the door," he yelled darkly.

Joel never stopped kissing his wife, but stepped into the library and slammed the door closed. "I hope you don't have any important papers on the desk," Rafe muttered.

"Why?"

"They might just do it on the desk, sweetheart," Rafe stated in a dark, frustrated tone.

"'It'?" She blinked, understanding now. "Not on a bed? Goodness, you mean that men can perform in places other than a bed? Well, I know Liam did, of course. There he was staked out, gagged, and Elizabeth—"

Rafe groaned, a raw frustrated sound, and she had the distinct impression he wanted to get away from her as he quickly lowered them to the floor.

"Oh, oh...got to go. I knew Duncan couldn't wait four days and we've only been here three. It's been fun. Call us if you need anything else," Sybil said as she began zipping her bag closed. "Fiona and Joel are upstairs packing now. Nick is warming up his helicopter."

Elspeth stood on tiptoe to peer out of the window. "Mmm. Snowshoes. How inventive. Only Duncan, Calum, Alek and Birk would have taken the over-the-mountain route. Alek said to take plenty of before and after photo shots."

Lacey stood on a stool beside her sister-in-law. "Yep. Way past time to go. Birk has that look. He wanted to come this summer with the baby and said that the meadow would make perfect camping. We could bring our tepees. All of us have them."

"Camping in the meadow, how delightful. You'll come back of course, won't you?" Demi asked and hurried to see what the women saw, what caused them to hurry, excitement flushing their cheeks. Four tall men stood outside the castle, their legs spread over snowshoes and their arms folded across their chests. Despite the greenery wilting in their hands, they looked immovable and fierce. "Who are they?"

"Husbands wanting wives. Duncan has no patience at all when I'm away. He's come to claim me and there is nothing more exciting than when he's like that," Sybil whispered in a delighted tone. "See those wilted flowers in his hand? That's his attempt at making nice when he's really determined to have his way."

Demi studied the men, all wearing scowls and carrying slightly crushed flowers. "They don't look happy. Oh, dear."

"They can't have their way all the time, and absence is good for the heart," Lacey said. "We can't let our husbands tell us what to do and what not to do, and we wanted to help you now, not wait until they could come ruin the fun and we had our babies underfoot. We'll be back, though, complete with children, when the weather is better."

"I cannot wait to get my hands on that man," Talia murmured, staring at Calum.

"Bye. It's been fun. Call us. Let me know if that legend pops up," Elspeth, an ordinarily elegant woman, said on her hurried, flustered way out of the kitchen door, followed by Sybil and Lacey. They each paused to kiss and hug Demi, who was stunned.

"I—" Demi stepped aside as Joel and Fiona each kissed her cheek as they passed her.

Caught in the wave of Tallchiefs all much taller than she, Demi reeled backward, only to be twirled, caught up in Nick's arms and kissed hard and quick. He replaced her feet to the floor and over her head, grinned boyishly at Rafe. Demi looked helplessly at Rafe, his arms crossed over his chest, a scowl on his face. He looked as grim and determined as the men outside. Demi smoothed her hair. "This is so fast. I feel like I'm caught in a whirlwind."

"Some things happen fast, others don't," he said in an unreadable tone. "They're waving to you," he reminded her.

Demi whirled and forced her hand to wave. "I love you all," she hurled into the March air, her heart filled with the warmth they had brought to her. They were her very own family and when they came back there would be children running through the halls of the castle and playing in the meadow, as it should be. She threw open her arms. "Come back."

"You're not going to cry, are you?" Rafe asked unevenly as she closed the door on the Tallchiefs. The sound of Nick's helicopter began to fade away.

"I've always wanted a large family and I do love them so. They're dearer to me every time I see them," she whispered, feeling wobbly and fragile as Rafe drew her against him, rocking her. She allowed the unfamiliar comfort. "I suppose you'll be leaving now. I want you to itemize a bill for supplies and labor and thank you for—"

"I'm not going anywhere, sweetheart," Rafe murmured against her ear. She wondered if he knew how closely and tenderly he held her, as if their flesh and lives would be forever one. His big hand smoothed her back. "And now, you're going to tell me what you're up to."

In his lifetime, Rafe had never cared whether people trusted him, but now Demi's soft gray gaze shielded her distrust. "I can't."

He wouldn't beg; he realized how much her trust mattered to him and that grated. "I see. Then I'll just have to stay until I find out, won't I?"

She turned to him, her expression desperate and her hand upon his chest. "If I tell you, will you go? Will you leave here and never say a word to anyone about my plans? Oh, please, Rafe, promise me that you will—"

Rafe glanced down at the small, capable feminine hand on his chest. He couldn't leave her, not until he understood how he felt. "I can't do that."

Demi's fist clutched his sweatshirt, then the other fist grabbed it and Rafe fought wincing as she caught the hair on his chest; Palladins were taught not to show pain. She tugged him down to her level. "Rafe, I'm desperate."

He wanted her desperate for him. "This point is nonnegotiable. You will tell me your plans, Demi."

While she wavered, Rafe picked her up and carried her into the library, sitting on her father's chair with Demi on his lap. She glanced fearfully at the too-neat stacks of paper on the desktop. "They wouldn't have—"

She looked up at him. "You can't hold me on your lap. I am not a child and there is no comforting to be done."

"Consider it just a thing one relative does for another." Rafe tried to force his body to relax; Demi's soft bottom fitted perfectly on his thighs. "We're going to talk this through...you're sewing until all hours, you're reading women's magazines and you're on a tight schedule. Why?"

Demi gripped his sweatshirt and again, Rafe tried not to wince. "My husband—ex-husband—is after the castle. He's trying to prove that since I'm my father's heir that the castle was marital property at the time of our divorce and he thinks he is entitled to a 'compensation.' He can't get it, of course. But just the thought that he is looking for legal loopholes frightens me. I would never, never marry again, or even come close to that pain again. Oh, Rafe, Thomas has no—"

"He's not getting the castle, sweetheart. Now explain your sewing—"

"I'm making underwear!" Demi wailed. "Lots of it. All sizes, petites to pluses. I want to sell it. Rafe, I'm giving sensuality seminars here in just two weeks and I don't have proper brochures printed or the place ready, and everything must be done. I've put ads in major city newspapers and taken applications for The Women's Sensuality Retreat. Four sessions, all four weekends in April...if all goes well, I'll make enough to pay off immediate bills and invest for more food and better accommodations—perhaps cots instead of asking them to bring their own bedrolls. I've always found that Father adapts well, once I have plans under way and they work. You won't call him, will you?"

Palladin, Inc.'s chief of acquisitions and product development sat very quietly, his hand resting on her hip. "You have a good solid plan. It should be successful...a retreat for women, discussing intimacy, selling lingerie."

Demi brightened, sitting up straighter on his lap. "I knew I could count on you to see how important it is to let me go about my business. I have to hurry, Rafe. I've got so much work to do and I know that you have a mountain of work waiting for you and you must miss your penthouse—Fiona said you had a beautiful one, though you travel so much you rarely use it...or perhaps you need to travel, you know...get out there on the road, churning profits—''

He was being dismissed and it hurt. For a man whose scarred heart was encased in steel, the admission was a shock. ''I could help you,'' he offered stiffly.

''I've hurt you.'' Demi's soft voice drove Rafe's shock deeper. Palladin men had been taught not to show their emotions.

She touched his jaw, smoothed it. ''I suppose you could teach me how to drive before you leave. Father isn't here and I—''

Waves of sheer delight slid through Rafe. Demi wanted him for something; she needed him. If she needed him for driving lessons, he could expand her need of him, step by step. He tried to keep his tone casual. ''I could teach you how to drive. If you're going to be a businesswoman in the country, you should know how to drive.''

An hour later, Demi almost killed his BMW, sailing it dangerously close to a pine tree. He hadn't meant to yell at her, but when he did, she turned and hurried into the castle. The drawbridge chains began creaking and it slowly, firmly lifted, sealing him from the woman he wanted to claim.

Rafe shivered, reining the need to scale the castle walls, find Demi and introduce her to his desire—which was obvious to everyone but her. He understood perfectly what Demi's great-great-grandfather, Tallchief, had felt about the Scotswoman he had captured, but who would not easily bend to his will.

Just then, Madeline arrived in her silver Range Rover and flung herself upon him, kissing him hungrily. While he tried to escape the flame-haired woman, Rafe heard the drawbridge lowering. Demi stood at the entrance, her arms crossed in front of her. ''You may bring your friend into my castle,'' she called. ''She'll have to pay lodging, of course.''

Five

"**H**ave you forgotten that your room is next to mine? Rafe is my relative, but guests sleep on the ground floor," Demi demanded coldly of Madeline that night, just as she was about to remove her skimpy peignoir and slip into Rafe's sleeping bag.

He'd been lying on the floor, wishing for Demi's soft body, her sweet kisses and wanting to cuddle her. For a man without a tender background, the new addiction to cuddling and a semi-continuous hardened, aching body was unnerving.

"This isn't what it looks like," he managed to say to the woman he wanted in his bed, directly under him or actively pursuing the "Vice Versa." Rafe studied Demi's small, taut curved body, her expression said she was ready to defend him. Rafe turned the thought: no one had tried to defend him since Joel—also a boy—had fought to protect him. This small, fierce woman seemed determined to unnerve him.

"Of course, it isn't what it looks like," Demi stated stiffly as a piece of paper floated out of her apron to rest on the floor.

"Come along now, Madeline. Your nice cozy paid for room is downstairs. There are no comforts up here."

"Oh, I think the comfort I want is right here." Madeline looked seductively at Rafe and allowed her black peignoir to drift off her bare shoulder. "He can decide. Tell her, Rafe."

Women. One wanted to have him—a reminder that they had had a previously loose relationship, and a cool slaking of their bodily needs—and the other woman—whom he desired—wanted to protect him. The paper that had fallen from her apron was probably another article that mocked his appeal to Demi, goddess of the harvest. Harvest. When had he last harvested? Or wanted to? He stared at Demi's naked, enticing ankles and knew that there was only one woman he wanted to harvest, to hold and stroke, nibble and—"Madeline, why don't you go along and Demi and I will set this straight."

Madeline sent Demi a sneer, tossed her long red hair and gathered her black peignoir around her short, racy lace teddy. "Later."

"How dare you!" Demi shot at Rafe the moment Madeline slammed the door. Heat steamed out of her, her voice trembled, emotions swirled around her like a mountain storm. "You cannot bring your mistresses here, and you will have to control yourself until you leave the premises."

"Will I?" In the next heartbeat, Rafe was out of his bedroll and had Demi pinned against the wall, his hands beside her head.

"You're naked," she whispered unevenly.

"I'm hungry," he whispered back. And to make certain that she understood perfectly, because Demi could take a hurried, wrong turn to his predictable, methodical path, Rafe added, "I want you, Demi."

"For what?"

With his body aroused, his heart racing with each scent, Rafe wasn't certain he wanted to outline the mechanics of his desire.

Madeline pounded on the other side of the door. "Just how long is this going to take? Martinis go flat, you know."

"Why does she want you so terribly?" Demi whispered un-
certainly.

Rafe's ego flattened; Demi had a way of shredding his past life.
Madeline wanted him for sex and only sex, not for tenderness or
sweet kisses, or anything else. Before meeting Demi, he'd wanted
a relaxed relationship and Madeline had fit that position. With
Demi, he wanted exclusive and long-term rights. It was just a
matter of putting everything in alignment and *getting her to notice
him as a man.* "We had an equal relationship. We both got what
we wanted."

"Oh. In my experience, it is the male in pursuit of the female—
oh...in matters of sex. Yet, Madeline is in pursuit. Don't you think
that is unusual?"

"Is that what your women's magazines say?" Rafe leaned
down to kiss the corner of her mouth. It was delicious. He kissed
the other side and then the tip of her nose.

"Not exactly. You see, women must prepare a receptive image
for the man they seek. It's all very intricate—"

He gently slid his hand up to her breast and watching Demi's
flush rise, Rafe enclosed her softness slowly.

She stiffened and inhaled, flattening her back to the wall. "Do
you love her, Rafe?"

"What?" He'd been concentrating on how lovely her breast
was within his hand, how soft and fragile and womanly. One
wrong move and he could hurt her— He realized he had just
trembled.

Palladins did not tremble. They brawled and fought when
needed, or coldly faced the task in front of them. But they did
not tremble.

"I will not be a substitute for her. I was once and—" Demi
bit her bottom lip. "I've found that in sensual matters, I'm lack-
ing. Thomas explained that very clearly to me. I realized while
reading all those articles how badly I miss the mark."

Rafe wanted to physically explain to her ex-husband how to

treat a lady. When Madeline pounded on the door again, Rafe said, "Madeline, I will talk with you later."

"Once you point out the innkeeper's proper duties, you can come to my room. It's shabby, but more comfortable," she called seductively. "I'll mix the martinis."

Rafe looked down at Demi's soft gray eyes and knew that he would never have a woman other than Demi. "I'm not going to her," he whispered and added, "now or ever."

"She wants you and she's beautiful," Demi whispered back, looking down to where Rafe was slowly unbuttoning her night-gown.

He shuddered when the black lace appeared, her breasts snuggling warmly inside. Unable to stop, Rafe bent to brush his lips across the creamy softness. Demi's hands had risen to his shoulders, her fingers rhythmically clutching and releasing. "You look very warm," she whispered unevenly. "Do you have a fever?"

Rafe fought groaning. "Trust me, Demi," he managed against her lips and knew he had to touch her tongue with his. The intimate slide and sensual play was little compensation for what he really wanted.

"This won't be like the driving lesson, will it? You yelled."

Demi patted the neat stacks of seminar booklets resting on the huge, long table in the main hall. Demi's Delites were neatly folded and arranged across the table, from size 7 leopard print to size 24 black and rosette, Sweet Dynamite. She glanced out the window to the peaceful snow-covered Rocky Mountains. Madeline had left in a huff and Rafe had been unapproachable for two days, glaring at Demi as if she had caused him pain. In those two days, he had made nonstop calls, drove his BMW into Amen Flats and returned with a huge beast of a pickup, loaded with a long smoothly finished plank table and sixteen matching chairs. Then he had slapped a crumpled article she had lost on it. "Sounds during lovemaking seem a little private to me," he had said, adding, "I don't know if it's healthy for women to practice those…those inside body exercises. You're not doing *that* in class, are you?''

The night that Madeline had arrived, Rafe's kiss had frightened Demi—because of what she felt stirring within her. She sensed that Rafe would not make love as hurriedly as Thomas, for Rafe was a slow talking, very certain and gentle man. Thomas had hurt her and Rafe seemed to take great care in how he drew her to him, how he placed his lips exactly on hers, his tongue gently entering her lips, her mouth.

She'd been inspired somehow, sucking him gently, and Rafe had begun to tremble, jerking her much closer and breathing unsteadily before he put her a distance away from him. There was just that heart-pounding moment when he looked down at her as though trying to make a huge decision. Then he had padded back to his sleeping bag, a tall man, rippling with power and something else. "Go away," he had said gently, despite his fierce, hungry look. "I'll deal with Madeline in the morning."

She had wanted to pet him, to soothe whatever dark pain rode him now. "You'll be nice, won't you? She is a paying customer."

"Damn it. I'm always nice," he had stated darkly, then he had turned his back to her. His body had actually shuddered as if in pain.

Now, a week and a half later, and planning the arrival of her first students, Demi checked her lectures on sensuality. They were outlined, businesslike, concise and logical. She was wearing her brand-new wardrobe investment—Western jeans, appropriately tight as the magazine models wore. She had had to lie down on the bed to zip them. Her new red sweater—red, because an article pointed out that men were alert to red—molded her body. She would dress the part—looking Western, intelligent and feminine. She had not yet braided her hair, and it flowed over her shoulders and down her back. She had a number of college degrees, excelled at data processing and could surely be a self-employed businesswoman—efficient, competent, moneymaking and logical.

Everything was logical but the way she wanted to leap upon

Rafe the first time she saw him in jeans, a flannel shirt and workman's red suspenders. He was stunning—tall, fit, a natural athlete with the wide red suspenders fitting his shoulders and down his chest. The suspenders affixed to his jeans' waistband in a manner that caused Demi to stand perfectly still, fascinated by the male beast prowling through her castle. Suspenders did wonderful things for Rafe's taut backside.

With a sigh she didn't understand, Demi forced herself to return to the business of making money. The ads would come out in the weekend newspapers in major cities. Aunt Nell would find some way to keep Nathaniel away for the entire month of April; she could not promise more. According to Aunt Nell, Nathaniel's health was already improving.

Rafe. He wasn't moldable, susceptible to her polite suggestions and simply moved her out of his way when he needed. He had tossed her upon her bed when she tried to support the other end of the board he was holding to make a shelf. The look that he had sent her as she lay sprawled upon the bed was fascinating— alert, predatory, hot and stirring.

Yes, stirring. She had been stirred and her emotions had answered, just as alert and predatory. She wondered if she didn't have literature's "vixen-lady" tendencies.

Rafe. He was a complex man, disturbed by shadows, and wary of her. If she stood too close, he eased away.

On the other hand, his kiss had been interesting. "Open your lips, sweetheart" was a raw, male command she hadn't heard before.

She touched her lips and shivered, remembering Rafe's mouth fitting methodically, exactly over hers. Then a movement at the window caught her; she looked outside to see Rafe riding a horse and wearing leather chaps, expertly herding cattle into the meadow.

Demi hurried out of the castle into the mid-March air. The day was filled with the sound of birds and snow melting and grass growing in the meadow. Though snow lurked nearby, a warm wind had melted that on the meadow and the bubbling stream meandered through the valley. Terror leaped into Demi; Rafe could hurt himself—fall off the horse, the cattle could charge him. Old stampede movies flashed through her mind, people trampled and lying— Demi stepped into her practical firemen's boots and ran toward Rafe, seated on his horse, one forearm resting across the saddle horn, the reins threaded between his fingers.

Demi stopped abruptly, aware that Rafe's green eyes had traced her flight from the castle. He sat on his horse—a huge chestnut, obviously male, coat gleaming in the sun. Demi placed her hand over her heart, which was racing from the cowboy image in front of her. The thick forest and rugged, snow-covered mountains provided a perfect background for the man on the horse. Rafe's black Western hat was well-worn and curved, propped to the back of his head; he was dressed in a flannel shirt, an opened shearling jacket and jeans that ran into battered Western boots.

There was nothing kind in his expression. The hard set of his jaw was darkened by stubble, his mouth a grim line; the fierce line of his eyebrows shielded a brilliant emerald look that began to heat Demi from head to toe. He focused slowly on her breasts, which were rising and falling rapidly from her run to him.

She pressed her hand to the fast beating pulse at the base of her throat. "I'm afraid you'll get hurt," she finally managed. "If you fall, you're so big that I don't know if I could drag you into the castle. I suppose I could call for help, though it would take some time for anyone to get here—"

His left eyelid twitched. "Come here."

"Oh, I see." Demi hurried to him, lifting her arms to him. "You need help getting down. Here—"

Rafe plucked her up and settled her across his lap.

Rafe had gripped the reins, threaded through his fingers. He tried to swallow, his heart kicking up into overdrive at the sight of Demi running toward him, her curvy body encased in tight jeans. Her breasts flowed and rippled beneath the red sweater, her hair flying in the wind, gleaming blue-black in the sunlight.

The terror in her eyes had startled him; it was for him.

She clung to him now, her fragrant hair teasing his cheek, her face tucked close against his throat. He tightened his arms carefully around her, fearing he would hurt her. Yet he trusted his gut instincts, the instincts that made him good at what he did— acquire and develop. All he had to do was package himself as a product she wanted; one who could dislodge whatever damage her ex-husband had done to her. Rafe planned to move Demi into a smooth, well-adjusted relationship where he could hold her every night in his arms.

Rafe brushed his lips across her smooth forehead and eased his coat off, tucking her into it. He lifted her hair free and wound a strand around his thumb, stroking the silky texture. "Do you believe in the Tallchief legends, Demi? The ones attached to the items of their great-great-grandmother's dowry?" he asked very carefully.

"Of course. They all came true, once the items were located. True love came to those who found the items and claimed them. I believe in love. It just isn't for me and I don't have a legend to my name. You've ridden a horse before," she stated slowly as the horse, Roy, moved to the nudging command of Rafe's knees.

Demi didn't believe she was suited for love. Rafe considered the thought. Demi definitely should have some man loving her. Her lips should be rosy with kisses and she should never have to worry about money and survival again.

"You've ridden a horse before," she repeated, looking at him for an answer.

Rafe thought of the hours he and his brothers had spent as teenagers on the ranch, after thoroughly testing Mamie's authority. The old cowhands had adored Mamie and hadn't let her grandsons get away with one wrong step. After returning from town, tipsy and full of themselves, the three Palladin boys had to work on the ranch all day before resting.

"I manage Palladin, Inc.'s ranch. Riding a horse is a necessity." He tugged her hand from the saddle horn and slid his fingers through hers. He wanted to take her to the Palladin ranch, install her in the ranch house's lush bedroom, which he had never used, and make love to her. At the ranch, Demi would not be worked until she dropped; she'd have every convenience and time to think about their relationship. She'd have time to notice him as a man who desired her, not as another male tucked into her care. He wanted her to pick him from the herd.

Why was it so important that she be happy? Why did the sunlight dancing on the tips of her lashes fascinate him?

Why did his troubled heart ease, just looking at her?

"I thought you were a businessman, with muscles that came from spas," she said softly, smoothing her hand over his upper arm. He startled himself by flexing his muscles, like a boy showing off for his first girl.

"I haven't had time for that or other things." The lush grass of the meadow needed calves and cows and colts and children. He inhaled unevenly, startled by his whimsical thoughts. Rafe Palladin did not run on whims or legends; he dealt with life and realities. What did the son of Lloyd Palladin know about loving children? About treating a woman tenderly?

Images of Lloyd's rough treatment slid through his mind. He eased his hand away from Demi's and she turned quickly to him. She reclaimed his hand between her two. "You've gone all dark and broody again. Don't. Just don't. Whatever is troubling you, I will help. I want you to tell me everything."

Rafe looked down at her earnest expression. No one had ever dared push him, prying into his life. "I don't 'share' myself," he stated stiffly.

"You'll have to learn then, won't you? If you're going to stay here, you'll have to learn to relate. You'll have to start telling me some of your feelings, not all, because I believe in privacy, but it is difficult having you glower at me and not understand what I've done wrong. Otherwise you're free to go, and I would prefer that you did that, anyway. You can't be sleeping very well on that hard stone floor.''

Rafe released the reins and held Demi close to him. He didn't feel nice and gentlemanly; he felt hungry and raw and fearful that a part of him would be like his father—cruel, abusive, unable to treat a woman with tenderness. "I've never liked ultimatums. You'd do well not to test me.''

"Threats?'' Demi's sleek eyebrows lifted warningly. "I do not react well to threats, and you're wrong. Your life is not your own—you have Joel, Nick and Mamie and more.''

Rafe wanted to toss the reins of his control into the March mud. A man had to fight to keep his pride around Demi. "I'd like to know if you like kissing me,'' he said stiffly, resenting that he had to drag any admission from her.

After a long silence in which his impatience rose unexpectedly, Demi looked up into the mountains and stated in a tone of a wine taster, "Warm. Friendly. Pleasant. Playful and with a touch of—''

"Sexual hunger?'' Rafe supplied after a moment of heart-starving desperation.

She looked at him blankly. "Good heavens, no. I know my appeal. Thomas explained in great detail why he had to turn to another woman.''

"I am a different man, Demi,'' he explained very tightly.

"True, but I would think that male tastes tend to run along the same line. I've never been able to flutter my lashes and act light-brained. I've always had to be competent and in control. I've always known exactly what was expected of me in order to protect those I love. Sexless, yes. That is what Thomas called me. Sexless and bookish. You have no idea how explaining sensuality to my classes has frightened me. I've given tons of seminars before, but always on handling masses of data, and nothing so whimsical and indefinable—you know, dealing with body chemistry, if there is such a thing. There's the matter of visuals, too—like putting a nice meal on china to make it taste better.''

She eyed Rafe speculatively as a hawk soared through the clean mountain air. "Madeline's appearance told me that you've had experience with sensuality. Perhaps you could give me input for my lectures."

He was just thinking of the input he wanted to deliver when her expression changed to delight. "Rafe, I have the most wonderful idea. If you have the time—and I know you are running your business daily—though you really should leave, and I have no idea why you are staying because you're not getting the castle— Yes, I do understand. You have pride, you gave a promise to my father to watch over me—a silly thing—but you did and you always keep your word."

She paused for breath and hurried on, "But do you...would you mind if I modeled my lingerie for you? You could give me quotes for advertising purposes. I wouldn't use your name of course. I know that a Palladin, Inc. executive couldn't possibly be used as a direct quote or a reference."

She cradled his face in her hands. "Oh, Rafe. You're the only male at my disposal. Please?"

"I'd very much like to be at your disposal," he returned formally as images of Demi's curved body dressed in tantalizing wisps of transparent fabric danced across his mind. She had trusted him with her plan; he was her guardian, but also the man who desired her. "Sweetheart, you want me to explore my feelings with you—"

"Yes, I do. I've always been really good at soothing men and helping them along their way. It's clear to me that you are even more delicate than my father or Thomas." She brightened and hugged him tightly, looking up at him expectantly.

Rafe almost groaned and looked down to where her softly curved red-clad breasts flattened against him. He did not feel delicate; he felt very hard. "Demi. Sweetheart. I don't think I'm ready for this just yet."

She patted his cheek, her expression one of understanding. "Keep trying. I'm a patient woman."

Rafe decided to toss away his pride and ask for one small tidbit

from her that would indicate she might cut him from the herd.
"Could you kiss me? I'm feeling—unsteady."

"See? Don't you feel better? You need reassurance—everyone
does at one time or another—and you've just told me your feelings." She raised to kiss his cheek and Rafe turned slightly, meeting her lips.

The meadow danced in sunlight as Demi held very still, Rafe's
hand smoothing her back beneath the heavy coat. Then she
slanted her mouth slightly and eased her arms around him. Her
tiny, soft kisses pressed a trail across his mouth and returned,
warmed by her uneven breath. She flicked her tongue along his
bottom lip and unused to being controlled or tasted, Rafe shuddered, parting his lips slightly. The tip of Demi's tongue played
with his and then slowly, tentatively entered into his keeping.
Rafe shuddered; he forced himself not to bear her to the ground,
to spread his coat upon the new grass and tear away his clothing.

She breathed unevenly, still kissing him, and reached to place
his hand upon her breast, moving restlessly against him. Her soft,
hungry purr destroyed him, and aching for her, Rafe slowly eased
up her sweater. "I want to look at you."

"Here? Now? Why?"

"There's not a soul around, honey, just you and me and the
birds and the 'why' is very personal and special to me." Did she
trust him?

"And the horse and the cattle. Oh, Rafe, I don't know how I
can manage cattle—" Demi sucked in her breath, her cheeks
warming, her gray eyes wide with shock as he cupped her breast.

"You're staring at me," Demi stated unsteadily a heartbeat
later.

"You're beautiful," he whispered with all the reverence filling
him.

Her body arched as his thumb brushed the black lace bra and
her nipples peaked. In another minute he'd—Rafe fought for control. He intended to treat Demi very carefully, not— He forced
himself to draw down her sweater.

"You're glowering," Demi stated as Rafe swept into the main hall that night, looking dirty, tired and furious. He'd been tightening up the old pickup's shed, unloading hay that Nick had helicoptered in, straightening old fence posts, stretching and fastening wire to them with a rough vengeance as though pitting himself against his frustration. The raw power in his movements and his gunfighter scowl at her told Demi that he did not want to be soothed.

He whipped his hat, dusty and lashed with hay, against his thigh, and braced his boots on the stone floors. "Oh, right. You would pick tonight for this," he muttered as he took in the pink camisole and dance pants she wore over her well-washed and paint-stained long johns.

"You've wallowed in your black temper all day, though I don't know why, and I forbid you to bring it into my castle," Demi stated righteously. "I am on schedule, but I cannot afford time spent with an ill-tempered male needing coddling, soothing and control."

That eyelid twitched again. "Is that what you think I need?" Rafe asked too quietly.

"My past experience tells me—"

"Oh, well, hell. You've got that, don't you? Plenty of experience?"

Demi clutched her notebook closer. Men in her life never argued with her, nor tested her decisions. "You want a brawl? A good argument? Very well. They sometimes clear the air—"

Rafe tossed his hat to a chair and walked by her on his way to the kitchen. She hurried after him. "Don't you walk away from me, Rafe Palladin."

She caught the shirt he hurled at her from the bathroom. "I know that you're upset about staying here and letting your business affairs slide. But you must realize that you are not getting the castle."

He ripped free his belt, jerked off his undershirt, flung it at her and began unbuttoning his jeans. "I do not let business slide. The damned castle is yours."

"You really should see about that eyelid twitch," she said as he sat and began pulling off his boots.

"It's a new development—since I met you." His hand covered the interesting line of hair from his chest and leading into his jeans. He glared at the hot pink lacy briefs draped around the shower to dry, then plucked them to throw at her. "Lady, you are in the bathroom with me and I'm about to remove my pants."

Demi clutched her new creations to her—size 8 to 20 in Moon Heat style, and realized desperately that she had never seen a full frontal view of a male—an interesting adult male—and that she had been waiting, holding her breath. "Oh."

His gaze ripped down her new creation in pink. "I like it. Looks fresh, bridelike. Sweet. Try it in black. Black is always good. White thermals beneath it probably don't help. Skin would be better, but oh, well, hell, I couldn't take that, could I?"

He stared at her brogans, closed his eyes and shook his head. Then he placed his hand gently upon her face and eased her back out the door, closing it firmly between them.

Demi clasped her hands together; she was delighted. Rafe had complimented her work. She leaned against the door and called, "You'll feel better after a good dinner."

"There's a full moon tonight. I'd like you to go outside with me, to check on the cattle. We could walk in the meadow," Rafe said, his tone formal. He stood in the center of the kitchen, long legs encased in jeans and his boots locked to the floor as if bracing for a shoot-out.

Demi finished stacking away the dishes, not too happy that Rafe had seared a huge steak to accompany her Greek salad, linguini and cheese dish. "I don't believe my schedule allows for—"

"Oh, well, hell. I wouldn't want to ruin your schedule," Rafe snapped, and slapped his Western hat against his thigh as he swept out of the kitchen.

Hours later, Demi had sewed miles of lace and silk and had designed a new leopard skin shortie nightgown. She felt like a huntress, and the material suited her mood. Once she had Rafe in her clutches, she was destroying him. No male ever walked out on a showdown with her—no male in her life had ever created the need for such a stressful battle.

In her life, Rafe equaled stress. *She* was always in control.

She heard his pickup door slam and hurried up the stairs to view the meadow in front of the castle. "So you're back."

She hurried down the stairs, primed to do battle. The draw-bridge was up and staying up. She paused to listen to the creaking chains, lowering the drawbridge. By the time she reached the main hall, Rafe was shouldering a huge mattress through the opened double doors. She watched while he unloaded the matching box spring and then easily carried in a frame and headboard constructed of huge, bark-stripped limbs. He paused outside the drawbridge to flick a rope from the turret above the drawbridge and wind it expertly as he stared grimly at her. Rafe shouldered by her to raise the drawbridge and ignored her tentative, "Rafe, are you feeling all right?" He flung off his coat and grimly began to pack his bed upstairs.

Demi prepared a cup of chamomile tea to settle her nerves. She decided it was wiser to gather her notes from the hall table, retreat to her bedroom and wait until Rafe was in a better mood to en-counter him. She settled the rose teacup and saucer on her bedside table, then snuggled down into bed with her notebooks and ref-erence books spread around her. She listened to the ominous quiet that stretched from Rafe's upstairs bedroom—his tidy, barren lair. Palladin, Inc.'s acquisitions and product development chief now had a desk made from sawhorses and planks. Demi tried to study her notes on "Ten Ways to Refresh a Tired Husband" and fail-ing, turned off her bedside light.

She smoothed her new Delites leopard nightie. No other man

had ever raised her temper to boiling, not even Thomas and his lofty declarations that he needed a "real woman." Demi had felt like hunting Rafe down tonight and—but those were primitive emotions, not within her usual realm, mere whims—

The door opened and Rafe stood outlined in the dim light, wearing his cowboy hat and boxer shorts, his legs braced apart as though readying for a fight.

"My bed is ready," he announced firmly, then glanced warily at the various styles of Moon Heat and Passion Prose and Sexy Sonnet draped around her room, waiting for Demi Delites tags to be sewn into them.

"Yes?" Should she have helped him put on the sheets?

Demi watched, horrified as Rafe came to her, flung back her blankets and scooped her up into his arms. "I like the leopard thing," he noted as he walked through the kitchen.

"You've been drinking."

"Two beers doesn't qualify. You're driving me crazy."

"Put me down this instant."

"You're mine. We need some ground rules before those man-hungry women arrive. Blast it, Demi, I'm the head of Palladin, Inc.'s acquisitions and product development branch. This project shouldn't be that difficult."

Stunned, Demi tried to find reality as he bore her upward to his room and kicked the door shut behind him. He dumped her into the black satin sheets of his bed, tossed his hat to the bedpost and climbed in beside her as if he'd been doing it for years. He briskly adjusted the expensive black-and-brown striped quilt around her shoulders and lay down beside her, his arms behind his head. "Don't be scared. I promised your father I'd take care of you and that holds, no matter how much I'd like to— Never mind."

"My students are not man-hungry," Demi said at last and shivered when her bare leg touched his rougher, muscled one beneath the satin sheet.

"And I'm not your ex-husband," he replied, reaching to tug

her down beside him when she started to fling back the covers. "I'll just come get you. And I'm tired, sweetheart. You could have mercy, just this once."

"I have been merciful to men all my life," Demi returned adamantly.

"'Merciful.' If we could just have sex, I think everything would settle down to a normal acquisition," he shot at her in a dark tone, laden with frustration.

Demi levered up to stare down at him.

"What?" His tone was flat, demanding. "Isn't sex on your tight little schedule?" Then he turned on his side away from her, presenting her with wide unbreachable shoulders.

Demi wanted to fling herself upon him, to rip away the restraints on her emotions and physically... She breathed unevenly, forcing herself to logically weigh her alternatives. She could leave him now. He'd given her that choice.

On the other hand, she wouldn't run from a fight and she was wearing the perfect Demi's Delite if she felt savage. Which she did; she just didn't know how to begin a primitive mode. She snuggled down in the luxurious black satin sheets and prepared for her next move. In her experience, battlefields could appear when the moment was appropriate. Perhaps this bed was her battlefield. She gripped the satin sheets in her fists; she wasn't leaving the battlefield to Rafe.

"I like your hair down. It's beautiful, like black silk," Rafe stated abruptly after a moment.

A thrill shot through her. Male compliments, according to her articles, when applied in a sincere mode, should be acknowledged. "Thank you. Your bed is lovely."

He snorted and she sorted through her memory banks to retrieve information on male snorts—the databases were empty. "I never shared a bed with Thomas," she whispered into the shadows. "This one is big, but you take up so much room."

Rafe's tall body stiffened as she continued, "We had twin beds and then separate bedrooms. I liked to read very late at night and that disturbed Thomas. Also, I'm a restless sleeper and my moaning sounds disturbed his sleep.''

"I see," he said, in a tone she could not determine. He turned slowly and his big hand slid to lay on her stomach. He rested his head on the satin pillowcase next to hers and looked at her. The moonlight passing through the windows stroked his lashes, softened his jutting cheekbones and slid over his lips, and touched the fascinating cleft on his chin. "I'd like you to sleep with me tonight."

She realized that the admission had cost him a measure of pride, this fierce man wrapped in shadows. She understood perfectly—he needed her, much as the other men in her life had needed her to understand and to comfort them. "Yes, of course."

His hand slid lower, rested over her intimately, his long fingers smoothing the leopard patterned silk between her thighs. "Afraid?"

And then he moved over her.

Six

Her ex-husband had hurt Demi badly, Rafe brooded as he slammed the hammer into the old square nails, sending them deeper into the shed's weathered wood. When he had moved over her, Demi had immediately stiffened. She clenched her lids closed as if preparing for a sacrifice, her body rigid. When he forced himself away, Demi had raced for freedom.

He slammed a new nail into the wood. Maybe he was like his father, an insensitive, selfish brute. The thought had weighed on Rafe for the next week and a half. He buried himself in rewiring the castle, building a one-sided shed for protection for the cattle, and spending his nights making up lost time by working at Palladin, Inc.'s ongoing business. Now it was Friday evening, and Demi's first guests were due to arrive any minute.

Rafe's project, *How to Acquire Demi,* wasn't running smoothly. He'd never worried about his sensitivity and now he realized that his skills needed honing, at least where Demi was concerned. He frowned at the rental bus unloading women in front of the lowered drawbridge. Fighting his own raging need for Demi and faced with her cold, rigid expression had been revealing—he had to find new tactics to make himself appealing to her. The problem was, he'd never had to work to make himself appealing; he'd never cared enough to take time to research himself as a product, one that wanted to be desired. He had accepted women as they evolved in and out of his life—except Sara Jane.

Sara Jane had reminded him of the pictures of Belinda, and when he'd found Sara Jane, battered and pregnant in that alley, he knew he'd protect her and her child from the man who had hurt her. He'd married her to disclaim all rights of her ex-boyfriend.

Rafe scowled at the woman snapping pictures of him. He began walking toward Demi, dressed in her Western jeans and wearing her red sweater beneath his chambray shirt. He liked her wearing his clothing and noted that she dressed in whatever came to her hand, which when he could manage, his shirts were available. Rafe snorted at his whimsy, his weakness to see Demi within the confines of his possessions. She was making his acquisition of her damned hard; he hadn't had to deal with his sensitivity before, and now she was destroying him. Damn it, he was fragile.

She struggled with the women's baggage, and Rafe reached to take it from her, hefting one up to his shoulder, tucking another under his arm, and carrying another in his hand. "I'd prefer that none of you allowed Miss Tallchief to wait on you," he said and because Demi was silently pleading with him not to run off her guests, he softened the command with his best smile. "So pick up those bedrolls and bring them into Tallchief castle."

He stopped in midstride as someone patted his backside. He turned slowly to the woman. "I don't come with the accommodations, lady," he said slowly, firmly, and glared at Demi, who he wanted interested in his backside and wasn't. Demi scowled at the two women sighing dreamily up at him as he toted the bags into the castle. What a man had to go through, just to cut the woman he wanted out of the herd.

Demi propped the binoculars up on the window shelf and found Rafe at the border of the woods, working to build a small shelter. He had locked his bedroom and deserted her. It was late Saturday morning, and she had delivered her Friday night sensuality lecture, followed by another—Setting Moods with Scents—at breakfast. Every time Rafe went by, carrying firewood for the upstairs bedrooms and the main hall, women turned to watch him.

They drooled...salivated and swooned and asked endless questions about the cowboy working on her ranch. "He's so gorgeous. Will he be here if I sign up for another course?" Phyllis, a thin woman topped by a mountain of blond, teased hair, had asked.

Rafe had slashed a harsh look at Phyllis and stared at Demi as he plopped two buckets of milk onto the kitchen table. "You can read what to do about this. You're good at 'reading' about how to do things, aren't you?" he had demanded in a dark tone that raised the hair on the back of her neck.

"He's just a businessman on vacation, you know—roughing it. I've been thinking about seminars for men. Lunch in an hour," Demi had called over Rafe's broad shoulder to the women watching them.

"Lady, I am spoken for," Rafe had mysteriously snapped and stalked out the door.

"Madeline, I suppose?" Demi had called furiously after him, shocking herself.

He had turned slowly on the drawbridge; he leveled a cool "let's have this out now" stare at her. Demi slammed the kitchen door between them, startled by her anger and jealousy. She didn't have time to deal with Rafe's challenges, nor did she want to— or did she? She plunged into making her retreat a success. The women had loved Demi's Delites and almost cleared out her inventory, buying for friends. She would have to sew frantically to prepare more for next weekend.

Now, in the lenses of Demi's binoculars, Rafe rode his horse toward the castle, dismounted and with a rope tied to his saddle horn, eased down into the moat. The calf trapped there bawled frantically to the cow above, who mooed back. Distracted from Demi's lecture on Seductive Looks, the ten women had hurried to the drawbridge, clearly in awe of the lean, powerful cowboy, easing hand over hand down the rope to save the calf. If Rafe didn't keep out of sight, she would never get the women into her Seductive Touches class. Demi had to succeed to save her father's dream.

Demi put down the binoculars, hurried to the bucket now filled with water and opened the window. She dumped it on Rafe. "You can't sabotage my classes, and ruin my income."

Rafe jerked his hat from his head and slapped the excess dampness from it with his leather glove. He glowered up at her, snagged the calf under one arm and yelled "Git" to his horse, who immediately started backing away, drawing Rafe and the calf to safety.

"This is great! It's an act—all a part of our fee. How wonderful!" one of the women called to the others, who screamed with delight as Rafe tramped across the drawbridge.

"Ladies," he said, tipping his hat to the women in standard Western greeting as he passed them. He wiped his muddy boots on the planks and then on the thick braided rug. His green eyes found Demi in the castle's shadows, pinning her, as he continued to walk toward her. "My lady wishes to speak with me alone. I'm taking her out for the afternoon. I'm certain you can do without us for a few hours."

One woman fainted, safely caught by her companions; the rest sighed. Demi hurried to her bedroom; she managed to lock her bedroom door, only to find it splintered from the hinges. Rafe walked through it, bent to flop her over his shoulder and walked out of the castle.

"How undignified," she managed to say while dangling from his shoulder and forcing a smile at the women who were sighing dreamily. Demi realized that she had never been in a position that she had to defend herself from a man who wanted her company;

she didn't know how to react and decided to flop along until Plan A came to her.

He patted her bottom and kept his gloved hand on her until he deposited her into his saddle. Rafe leaped up behind her, gathered her safely into one arm, and with a clicking noise to Roy, he began to ride from the meadow. The women sent up a delighted cheer.

"This isn't part of any act," Demi muttered, turning toward Rafe. She removed her nose from the warm, enticing hair at the base of his throat. "I'm furious with you, you know. You are destroying my seminars. I know that you want me to fail, to have to sell to Palladin, Inc. Well, I won't fail. You have no idea how absolutely brutal I can be when I want something."

He snorted, infuriating her further. "Snorting is not a language-defined sound."

Rafe had no idea what he was going to do with Demi, but he wasn't letting all those women have her. He wanted her talking with him—about sensuality, and doing something with what she had learned. His current fragile state wasn't that easy to bear. "You've been running and fetching for those women for a day and a half. You look tired."

"Well! Thank you very much. You could return to acquiring things for Palladin, Inc. and leave me alone."

"I am acquiring what I want and damned soon." Rafe held the birch branch away from Demi's head as the horse passed by it.

"You can't have the castle. You can't just come in, flop me over your shoulder and take me away from my business. You broke down my door...tore the hinges from the frame and...you broke down my door." Her voice rose indignantly, and chipmunks scurried from the path of his horse.

"I'm a cad," he muttered. "I miss you," he added, resenting the truthful statement, and gathered her closer to him.

"Oh, I see." Demi placed her hand over his on her stomach. She looked down at his fingers, splayed open and possessive—

not at all like Thomas's fingers-together touch...not that Thomas ever held her so closely, usually just for photos. Much like he'd hold a book. "I know you're fighting your past, Rafe. It's easy to see that something is bothering you. Of course, I can spare a few hours for you."

"Gee, thanks."

Despite his frustration, Rafe settled back to enjoy riding through the April sunlight with Demi in his grasp. The horse trail wound through the firs and pines and Demi pointed to Tallchief Mountain. "I still don't see how she could have become intimate with a man on her first meeting. Oh, I know Elizabeth had to save their lives, but still how did she know how to make him...you know—"

Rafe forced himself not to groan. "Could we ignore Elizabeth's athletic endeavors?"

"Well, I suppose." Demi studied the bubbling creek, bordered by aspens, sumac and pine. "Where are we?"

"That's one of the best fishing holes anywhere," Rafe said, swinging down from behind her.

"Ah! You like to fish. You've apparently been under a strain. That is supposed to be good therapy."

Rafe placed his hands on her waist to lift her down and knew exactly what therapy he needed.

Rafe, standing, legs braced, stripped down to his T-shirt, whipping the fly expertly over the shimmering water, fascinated Demi. Spring sunlight filtered through the pines and the new aspen leaves, dancing upon the water. He concentrated on each whip of his line, which created huge S shaped designs over the water, his free hand working the line.

"I think we could be friends," she called as she sat cross-legged on the blanket near him and a bird shot through the cold spring air.

"No."

"You really shouldn't break down doors. You could get hurt."

He continued swirling the beautiful designs of the fly fishing line over the water. The sunlight glinted on the muscle crossing his jaw as it contracted and released. He looked totally isolated, hoarding his thoughts.

"I see you've caught several and they seem to get away, just as you take them off the hook. If you need help, I'm available. My father and Thomas tried to fish and I took their fish off the hooks," she offered. "I dug worms and put them on their hooks."

"No."

"That's a nice high-tech, collapsible fishing pole," she said, hoping to soften his mood. "Is it a Palladin, Inc. design?"

Rafe slanted a look at her, and with a snap, collapsed the pole, placing it into a compact case with an assortment of fly lures. "I will not teach your ladies how to fish," he stated, sprawling on the blanket beside her.

"The sun is really nice. Warm," Demi noted shakily when he continued to stare at her. She didn't trust the lazy dark green depths of his eyes, as though he knew something she didn't.

"When I take you, sweetheart, I'd really prefer that you did not lie there like a human sacrifice." He chuckled and stroked her hot face. "You could lie on me."

Demi shredded the leaf in her fingers and shivered when Rafe's fingers toyed with her braids, freeing them from on top of her head. He touched the tip of one, crossed her breast and stroked it with his finger. "I married Sara Jane because she needed me. She'd been battered and she was three months pregnant and terrified what her boyfriend would do if he knew about the baby. He had unsavory associates and I wanted to give her my full protection, making certain there was no question about Robbie's father. I married her—it was that simple. I took financial responsibility for her and Robbie and they were safe. It worked. I liked having them close when I was home. Robbie is special. He always was. But I knew that one day she would fall in love and she has. She's very happy with her new husband, so is Robbie."

"I see. That was a noble gesture." Demi glanced at the sunlight shimmering on Rafe's dark brown lashes. She barely kept her finger from stroking them.

"My father had left enough broken women behind him. It seemed appropriate that I help a girl like Sara Jane. I had the financial means and I liked her." There was a quick frown as if something painful had touched his heart and then Rafe smiled, one of those disarming boyish smiles that could make her heart leap. He tugged her braid. "Don't think my nobility applies to you, sweetheart. When it comes to you, I'm very selfish."

His fingers toyed with her top button, then slid it free. His look was dark, intent and wary. "Come lie upon me, sweetheart."

"I'd rather not. The blanket is fine." Years of reserve cloaked Demi's desire to throw herself upon Rafe, to pin him to the ground and see if Elizabeth's "Vice Versa" really worked.

Rafe's large hand caressed her back lazily. "When you're ready," he murmured and with a sigh, closed his eyes. He lay there, huge, warm, waiting and delicious.

Demi shuddered. She wanted to shove up his T-shirt and place her breasts against his chest. "Thomas preferred to make love with our nightclothes on."

Rafe snorted and his hand slid beneath her sweater, warm fingers stroking her skin. "I wish you wouldn't snort. I can't tell whether it is an affirmative or a negative sound. It makes conversation difficult," Demi said as he hooked a finger on her jeans waistband, drawing her nearer.

"Do it," Rafe ordered without opening his eyes. "Whatever is making those gray eyes widen, your cheeks turn pink and your hand tremble, just spare yourself and do it. Take a chance, Demi. Follow your impulses."

She'd had to move carefully through life, protecting her father, taking care of her mother, and keeping everyone safe; she couldn't afford leaping into chances or taking what she wanted.

"It's not dark," she noted very properly. She remembered Thomas's hurried skirmishes in the dark bedroom, beneath the sheets, and always scheduled for eleven o'clock on Saturday nights and then not at all. "Not even shady. We're in full sun."

"Mmm. Have you ever sunbathed in the nude?"

"I've read about the benefits, but good heavens, no."

Rafe's lids opened slightly and a smile lurked on his mouth. "So proper."

The challenge sizzled around her for a moment and then Demi defied him, tearing off her sweater and letting the sunshine flow upon her skin. Rafe hadn't noticed, his eyes closed. So much for her allure. "I can be dangerous," Demi stated in her own defense. "I can," she repeated when Rafe chuckled.

She flung herself upon him and with him pinned beneath her, his hands on her bottom, she stated the obvious, "I will not be challenged, Mr. Know-It-All Palladin."

She'd never been athletic or wanted to physically pit herself against anyone; she'd simply plodded through what she was expected to do. Demi forced herself to breathe quietly, her heart racing wildly. She wanted to wrestle with Rafe, body to body, and revel in her strength. She shivered as his hands caressed her bottom.

There was nothing sweet or boyish about the man looking up at her. She didn't feel sweet either. They stared at each other and she realized that Rafe's body had tensed, hardened and that a distinct masculine shape had arisen between them, shielded by layers of denim and cloth. "My," she whispered breathlessly.

"Yes, 'my.' I respond to you, sweetheart, and that is a fact." Then Rafe slowly drew her head closer and brushed a kiss across her lips. "Ready to go back?"

Rafe spun the top on his Palladin, Inc. desk. Very old, splashed with hot pink petals, Japanese symbols and perfectly balanced, the top's spinning motion mirrored his thoughts, which always circled back to Demi. Rafe slowly placed his finger on the exact center of the top, stopping it. He had his pride; Demi barely noticed him as she plunged into sewing and running her weekend retreats; the last two weekends he'd escaped back to his Denver office, pretending to work.

He studied the crystal lying on the desk, which somehow reminded him of Demi—and ran his fingertip along the smooth, cool, almost untouched surface.

The nagging truth was that he needed Demi and he wasn't too certain what his bargaining potential was as a desirable male. Demi had not made one move to acquire him. That nettled.

He unbuttoned his vest and rolled back his sleeves.

He wound the cord around the top. On the other hand, as the son of Lloyd Palladin, a brutal man, Rafe should know better than to come close to Demi's innocence. He didn't have a heart to offer her, not a sliver of sensitivity, and in the end, he would hurt her.

Rafe spun the top again and it circled the neat stack of business folders waiting for his attention. He'd placed the matter of his birth mother in a mental drawer; his fascination with Demi had overridden everything else. Once the matter of Demi and his relationship was under control, he would decide what to do about Belinda's letter.

Demi's outdoor lecture on women's and men's orgasms and intimacy had carried across the meadow to him as he was building a henhouse. He'd been cutting boards and when she had finished her blithe and experienced sounding lecture on holding the male body very tightly in the last throes, Rafe discovered that the boards had been cut too short. She didn't lecture about foreplay, rather ''prelovemaking exercises.'' The slow lip-moistening technique and flirtatious glances class had caused his body to lurch into red-alert.

The only male on the premises—other than the rooster and his gelding, Roy—Rafe had felt delicate and endangered. Escape came in the form of a Palladin business disaster and he had hurried back to Denver.

The woman wearing the huge sombrero, spandex and silver boots had patted his bottom as he had passed. Another woman had crept across the meadow at night and tried to crawl into his tiny cabin's window. Rafe snorted and studied his top collection, which spanned several walnut shelves in his office. He seemed to appeal to women—except to Demi. To her, he was just a...a fixture, an unwanted one who she feared might rip her castle away from her.

He regularly called Nathaniel, who was having a wonderful time examining old conquistador scrolls in Arizona, owned by a private collector and a friend of Nell's.

Rafe spun the antique Japanese top again. Demi had been too happy and busy to notice that he brought her tea at four o'clock every afternoon.

Tea. He was no more than a damned, unwanted butler and he resented those pats on his head as she passed; he wished they were lower and more intimate.

That had rankled and Rafe had slunk back to his ultraexecutive office lair to lick his wounds. On his intercom, Mamie's light blinked and Rafe pushed that button. "Rafe."

He scanned the modern glass and chrome executive office, looked across Denver's skyline to the mountains and sighed, wishing he could hold Demi. He smoothed the desk and wished for her upon it.

"You've signed your name on the wrong line on the Hayes contract, Rafe. This is a first for you," Mamie stated in her crisp business tone. "When do I get to meet this girl?"

He spun the top and thought of the way Demi looked when she cuddled the baby chicks against her. She'd beamed up at him as though he'd given her sunshine. He'd wallowed in her delighted giggles, the chicks peeping in her arms. Demi was a woman who needed children and someone to take care of her—specifically him. She had the grayest eyes; sometimes they looked like mountain storms and other times like clear sky, and other times like hot or icy steel. She fascinated him. He reached over and punched his sound system. Mantovani provided excellent background to think about Demi. Sunlight passed through the windows to dance upon the crystal, shooting its rainbow of colors over him. Rafe stroked it and wondered whimsically if he could compose a sonnet. He'd learned to structure a business letter; a sonnet couldn't be that difficult. "What girl?"

"The one who has you going in circles. This is the first time you've failed to come back with what I wanted. I read that bull about leaving them alone, that the Valerians were happy. I make it my business to know what goes on in you boys' lives. What are you doing here? Get out there, make yourself appealing to the girl and marry her before you ruin my business. Do something romantic. It seems to me that the head of Palladin, Inc. acquisition and product development should be pretty creative when he wants something. I love you, by the way. What's that I hear? Mantovani?"

"Mind your own business. I love you, too," he snapped and clicked the intercom off to silence Mamie's laughter.

Rafe rolled back his sleeves and set upon the waiting paperwork. He noticed the coffee his secretary had placed on his desk. He wondered if he had ever thanked her for the many things she did to make him comfortable. "Thank you. Mrs. Jones? Did you enjoy the seminar at the castle?"

His fiftyish secretary's eyes lit behind her big lenses. "Oh, thank you for sending me. Just as you instructed, I was very careful not to reveal that I work for you. My visit was just lovely. My husband is just thrilled with— Never mind. Miss Tallchief is a wonderful workshop leader. She certainly seems to have sensuality under control...you just snorted, sir. Are you feeling all right?"

Demi curled on Rafe's bed, inhaling his scent. She turned over on her stomach, slowly spreading upon the bed, latching her hands and toes on the farthest corners she could reach, as if to capture the man and keep him in her grasp. She'd made more money than she'd expected and for two days, she'd hurried to pay bills and to catalog shop for castle items like braided scatter rugs and more material and Demi's Delites garment tags. Her father was enjoying the Arizona sunshine and it was only the first week of May. Her dream—rather her father's dream—was safe.

She missed Rafe. He'd looked so dark and ominous when she lectured out in the meadow, the sound of his hammer angry in the last weekend of April.

Demi rolled to her side, ran her fingers through the small warm patch of sunshine on the bed, thought of the crisp warm hair on Rafe's chest and studied the pines on the mountain outside the open window. All she had to do was pick up the telephone and call Rafe. Then what?

Tell him that the chicks were growing nicely and by summer she hoped to make her own egg noodles with their eggs? Tell him that the wildflower seed he'd planted on a barren stretch was doing well? Tell him how much she needed to see him?

Tell him how much she loved to see him eat those huge, working-man meals, loaded with butter that she had churned and bread that she had baked? Tell him that she loved every minute with him? Tell him that he should be kinder to himself?

"Call me if you need anything, and don't forget to milk the cows" when issued in a dark growl didn't exactly qualify as sweetness. Nor did the slam of the door as he had stalked outside to his BMW, dressed in his striped gray business suit. He'd looked at her sharply, glanced at his wristwatch and sped away as if hurling from the sight of her.

Demi rolled Elizabeth's crystals on her palm and they caught the sunshine in a myriad of light, sending blues and reds dancing across the room's ceiling. Demi ran her finger over the broken jagged edge of what looked like the base of a missing crystal. Elizabeth's letters had mentioned the crystal cave and Liam's gift to her, an English lady who had jewels far more than he could afford. She had written in her diary, "When my lover, the father of my son, my own dear Liam, came to sweep me from the Montclair hunting lodge, he brought the crystals. I was furious then as he pulled me from everything familiar and what I loved, packing me off like he owned me. But later, he gave me a choice to return to England and by then I knew I loved him. Love was in his eyes and his touch and the sound of his voice, rather than the words he spoke. I quite simply gave him my heart.''

Demi listened to the wind sweeping through the May air, carrying the scent of pines to her. She frowned and clutched the crystals; Rafe had not been able to capture her castle and so he had gone. Left. Taken his dark moods and heart-stopping boyish grins and stuffed them into his BMW without a backward glance.

He'd called twice in the two days and after asking a list of practical questions about her business and safety practices, unexpectedly asked her what she was wearing. His voice had sounded strangled when she told him—a new little design supported with elastic and matched by briefs. ''Uh huh. 'Surrender.' Uh-huh. Don't forget to pull up the drawbridge at night,'' he'd said before the telephone line clicked off.

Demi inhaled sharply and traced the broken stub of a crystal. She should be exhausted. She'd sewn every scrap of material and ordered more, she'd scrubbed the castle and studied her lectures, and missed Rafe.

She was in her element, tending other people's needs, nurturing and generally finding her place in life. Her students had sent delightful letters, full of praises and they were recommending her seminars to their friends. May and June Women's Sensuality Retreat seminars were already filled and applications for July were arriving. Her discount for successful referrals was working.

Tallchief castle, this land where Elizabeth and Liam lived, was now her home. Rafe had helped her to succeed, to wrest the castle from debt. He had looked at her so hungrily—he had touched her so beautifully. How could he walk out without so much as a handshake?

Demi frowned at the shadows and wished she were close enough to Rafe to scold him on his bad manners. After an air slicing noise, a thud sounded on the outside of the wooden shutter. She carefully stuffed the crystals back into the velvet bag.

Clutching it, she leaped off the bed and hurried to the open window. Embedded in the wooden shutter was an arrow with paper tied to it.

Rafe, dressed in his Western hat, denim jacket, jeans and boots, stood on the ground below. He held the reins to Roy and another horse, both with saddles and heavy saddlebags. His bow was slung from his saddle horn and with his arms crossed and wearing a scowl, he looked—sweet, she decided.

Delighted with the sight of the man she had missed desperately, Demi pried the arrow loose, gripped it and the crystals' velvet bag and hurried down the stairs, across the main hall and across the drawbridge.

"You're wearing my shirt," Rafe noted as she came to a breathless stop in front of him. He looked down the length of her body, draped in his shirt to her knees, and down her jeans to her brogans.

"I'm sorry...I— Why are you here? I thought you had pressing business." She loved the sight of him, all tall and rigid and wary looking. She reached to touch the darkened circles beneath his eyes and he jerked away as if she would burn him. For all his contrariness, acting like a lone wolf without a friend, she still cared about his health. She stroked her fingertip down the line between his eyebrows. She wanted to hold him in her arms, soothe him and— "You look tired. Haven't you slept?"

He glared down at her, the shadows of his hat making his green eyes seem as hard as emeralds. "Let's go."

Demi placed her hand across her heart. "Where? I just can't leave. There are the chickens and cows to tend, and Rafe, come inside and let me cook dinner for you."

He scanned the mountains, looking every inch like a Westerner bred for taming the land. "We're losing light."

"Oh."

Rafe slowly looked down at her as if gauging her for a fight. His left eyelid twitched just once. "Nick is flying in to safeguard the castle. He's fed a chicken or two in his life and milked cows.

You're free, if you want to come with me. If not—'' He shrugged, dismissing his feelings one way or the other.

The invitation wasn't exactly charming, but to Demi— She clasped the arrow tightly. ''You shot this, didn't you? Just like Liam—''

Rafe took the bow from his saddle horn, snapped it and instantly it collapsed. He tucked it into a tube and slid it into his saddlebags. His quick look away and the dark flush rising up his cheeks told her that he didn't want the matter pursued. Instead he took the arrow from her hand, carefully folded the paper and tucked it into the other horse's saddlebags, and replaced the arrow to the quiver. Then he bent and plucked a wildflower, tucking it into her braids, wound over her head.

She would have followed him anywhere.

''I just can't get over myself, how I just came with you, and you haven't said a word all day. I want you to know that I am thrilled, just the same. I've never indulged in spur-of-the-moment escapades. I'm just not a whim person. Our budget has never allowed an unplanned schedule. I've never been camping before. Why are we here?''

Seated and braced against his saddle, his legs in front of him and fully dressed, Rafe looked at the woman across the campfire, snuggling down in her sleeping bag—her single sleeping bag without him in it. It was Palladin's new model, the kind that allowed the zippers to unite and form a double sleeping bag. Demi trusted him when he didn't trust himself; there was nothing more he wanted than to meld those two separate zippers together the same way he wanted to fit their bodies together.

The camping trip was meant not only to please Demi, but to get her away from work. He wanted her all to himself.

She smiled at him. ''You're a wonderful guide. I had no idea you could make biscuits and cook fish on the campfire—wasn't that monster I caught the biggest fish you ever saw? Imagine living off the land, just as the Native Americans did.''

Demi had ignored the obvious. Palladin, Inc.'s affordable and complete camping gear made life much easier than the Native Americans' way of life. She looked like a child, dressed in Palladin's new pink line of women's matching sweat suits. It pleased Rafe to choose her garments, and he'd pleased the clerks by selecting a full Palladin Sportswoman wardrobe.

Rafe didn't like prowling through his guilt. She trusted him and he was on a mission to seduce her into a long-term, sole proprietorship adult and very physical relationship.

Demi sighed happily and stretched her hands upward. "Just look at those stars, as if you could reach out and touch them. It was just on a night such as this that Elizabeth managed to—you know...do that to Liam. Exactly how do you think he felt?"

Rafe closed his eyes and tried not to picture Demi over him. While they were riding, his body had ached every time he glanced at her lush hips in the saddle, her breasts flowing softly with each bump. She did look like a harvestable goddess, lush and ripe and perfect.

"I missed you," she whispered across the distance of the campfire and alarmed, Rafe almost spat out the last sip of coffee. He swallowed it manfully. Every molecule in his body told him to take Demi and make her see how logical it was that they belonged together...physically.

"Rafe?"

"What?"

"Did you miss me?"

The quiet, tentative question unnerved him. Missing wasn't an activity that he understood. It just hadn't entered his life that often. In Denver, he was uncomfortable with his need to be with Demi. He wasn't used to thoughts of a woman destroying his business life and his sleep. Once, after Demi understood just how feminine and appealing she was to him, their relationship would course along much smoother. Rafe stood suddenly and flipped his sleeping bag to lie next to hers. "We can talk better this way."

Demi smiled warmly. "I see. We wouldn't want to frighten the wildlife, now would we?"

She turned from him suddenly. "You may undress now. I know you like to sleep without a nightshirt."

So good old Thomas had worn a nightshirt; the thought grated. Rafe undressed down to his shorts. "Are you warm enough? Mountain nights can get very cold."

He closed his eyes and saw Nick and Joel snickering. Rafe was just one step away from the running out of gas routine to get close to his girl—who trusted him.

He slid into his separate bag, like a turtle sliding into a protective shell.

"Where are we going, Rafe? I suppose you've taken women camping before, since you seem quite apt at having guest facilities." Demi turned to him and her hand rested on his chest. He placed his over hers and raised it to his lips. The fingers on his other hand tapped rhythmically on his thigh.

"I've never taken a woman camping before." He resented the admission; he'd never *thought* about mixing women and camping, or choosing their clothing, thinking about making them happy. "We're going to a smaller, easier reached version of Liam's crystal cave. I thought you might enjoy it. The real one is too dangerous to reach. Generally I thought we were both due for a vacation. How's the Women's Sensuality Retreat going?" He picked a safe topic for discussion. Or was it?

"Marvelous. I'm all ready for this weekend. May and June are filled. July applications have started to arrive. By the time my father arrives, he won't be disturbed at all by using the castle to make money. Oh! Oh!" Demi scrambled across him, her knee hitting a vulnerable place on his body. She reached for her saddlebags. "I forgot to read your note."

While Rafe shifted uncomfortably, she carefully uncurled the note and the perfect crystal he'd kept all these years tumbled into her palm.

Rafe waited. The effort at courting her was dumb, laughable, and any woman in her right mind—

"You're so sweet." Tears came to Demi's eyes as she gripped the crystal and scanned his drawing. "Why, Rafe. You're quite the artist. I love it. How beautiful. Rather than using the Montclair crest, we'll use this design—a banner and behind it, an upright sword and an arrow crossing it. You're a genius, Rafe. No wonder you're the head of Palladin, Inc.'s acquisition and product development branch. I'm really sorry you failed in your mission to acquire the castle. I hope your grandmother won't be too disappointed."

"I've changed my priorities. She'll understand. Flexibility has always been part of business." He'd been called inflexible, but for Demi, he'd make an exception.

Demi carefully tucked the note and the crystal into her saddlebag as if it were a treasure. Rafe inhaled, wallowing in the small burst of pleasure; he'd succeeded in making her happy. He studied the soft firelit sweep of her cheek, her eyes shining at him.

Her look stunned him. It adored, treasured him. It placed him on a pedestal he did not deserve. He was on a mission to seduce Demi, not to be adored.

Seven

Rafe stopped abruptly, stunned by the image before him—Demi, nude and sunbathing on a large flat mountain boulder. Spread upon the red, jutting rock under the cold, clear blue sky, she looked like a delicate morsel—like the goddess of the harvest, waiting for him to... His mouth dried at the sight of her curved pale body, the taut rose-tinted buds on her breasts, the dark nest of curls between her thighs. He swallowed tightly before placing the bucket of water on the nearby rock and asking cautiously, "Demi, what are you doing?"

Without opening her eyes, she clamped one arm over her breasts and flattened the other over her femininity. That intriguing view left Rafe eyeing her pale lush curves—a flattened lower curve of her breasts, the neat dip of her waist, hips he wanted to grip in both hands. Her hair flowed around her head like a blue-black silken river, rippling across the stone. The gentle mountain wind toyed with the ends, lifting them until Demi appeared to be lying in a silky mound of feathers...until she shivered. "It is cold—refreshing up here, but what better time to try sunbathing à la nude. I read about this and liked the idea. Native Americans did not have our lush, soft towels...you know, I have never felt so much at peace, as if I have finally come home.''

Rafe forced himself to suck in the mind-clearing cold mountain air as she slowly removed her concealing hands, placing them straight at her side. ''Here we are, roughing it, faced with the challenges of survival at every turn. I feel like a pioneer. My sense of euphoria is almost intoxicating and I feel...yes, I know that I am unappealing, but with the sunshine on my body, I feel almost like a sensual woman. I keep thinking about poor Elizabeth, saving them all. Liam should have been grateful, you know. She saved his life, too.''

''I don't want to hear any more about Elizabeth's rescue. You'll catch cold,'' Rafe stated sharply. He dragged his gaze from Demi's taut, uptilted nipples and forced himself to look at the hawk soaring overhead, at the wind stirring the pine boughs, at the chipmunks racing up the red-barked trees—anywhere but at Demi's creamy white body. His own body felt as hard as the rock he stood upon.

Demi turned to him, shielding her eyes against the sunlight. ''Why, Rafe. You're embarrassed. Your face is flushed and you're looking everywhere but at me. Do you think Elizabeth hurt Liam when she, ah, you know...Rafe? You just cursed. I heard you, and you really shouldn't be such a prude, you know. Sensuality comes from knowing one's own body, enjoying it— Oh, that's right, turn and hurry away, just flee. Obviously you don't want to learn from my seminars on exploring the body with one's own touch. Take yourself away from my rock. Go on, shoo.''

''Your eyes are very green, almost emerald color, set in those dark lashes. When you're angry, they seem to almost shoot green fire, and then there's that lovely jade tint when you're in your softer moments. They were the green fire shade when you came tromping across my rock to cover me with that opened sleeping bag and then stuffed me into my clothes. But then you were probably just sensitive because I had noticed the—well, you know, your obvious below-the-belt problem. I'm sorry I stared.'' Demi picked at the rabbit Rafe had roasted over the campfire and settled for eating the baked potato. The night was unseasonably warm and she was wearing his chambray shirt, her legs crossed in front of her, her skin glowing in the firelight. She frowned at him, and raised to wipe his chin with the edge of a towel.

Then she patted him on the head.

The gesture took him to the level of a favorite pet, or a boy drooling for a woman. Rafe grabbed her wrist, and tugged her into his lap. In surprise, she arched back and they rolled onto the sleeping bag. "I want you," he heard himself rasp.

He had no time to listen to the imaginary guffaws of his brothers. He, Rafe Palladin, Mr. Cool and emotion free was desperate for the woman who had been driving him nuts with her touches to her breasts—she was taking her own advice and touching herself lightly, sensually.

And because he was afraid she would ask an innocent question that would shame him further, he sealed her lips with his—gently, because he wanted her to know how much he treasured her.

Demi shivered, her gray eyes wide when he lifted his head. "Off," she ordered shakily, her cheeks pink in the firelight.

Rafe took his pain and rolled away. He had disgusted himself; he had about as much tender technique as a—as Lloyd would have had. His dark legacy and pounding desire mocked him.

His borrowed shirt discarded, Demi's bare breast dragged softly against his arm until she leaned over him. He turned slowly to her, her shoulders bare in the firelight. "I think you're wonderful," she whispered, easing closer to his bare chest. "Please take me."

In the warm double-zipped sleeping bag, while the moon rose over the mountains, Rafe touched her slowly, reverently, as if she were made of wildflower petals, and dew on the morning spider-webs.

Rafe's kisses soothed, warmed and kept returning to her lips as if he could not leave her. His hard hands skimmed over her, finding the hollows of her body, his thumbs traced her hipbones, fingertips circled her navel, caressed her back. All the gentleness she had ever known seemed to come floating to her on a muscled, very male and sweet cloud.

Yet the heavy pounding of Rafe's heart told her that he wanted her. She prayed that she wouldn't disappoint him as she had Thomas.

She never wanted Rafe to leave her, his tall body trembling, warming to her touch, every cord taut and muscles flowing and—he was so dear, so susceptible to her self-touching, staring hungrily as she ran her finger down her throat.

Demi placed her open hand on his bare bottom, taking what she wanted for once in her life. Her notion of greed for Rafe rose, fed by each soft caress, each touch.

In the shadows, she caught the flash of the foil package and knew that he would take care of her.

Then he returned to her, his mouth teasing hers gently. His fingers slid within her intimately and she gasped, unprepared for the warmth filling her, the moist heat devouring her. Then she was stretching, Rafe entering her, trembling over her, kissing her softly, sweetly, easing his body into hers....

"This doesn't hurt," she whispered against his lips as he waited for her to adjust.

"You're very...tight, but so—no, it shouldn't."

Demi tried to push away the images of Thomas's crude, hurried lovemaking. "He didn't make love at all," Demi stated with the first real tug of anger against Thomas. "Why, he never even—Rafe, the man was my husband and he actually never...never...tasted me. He fumbled, and my inability to become aroused was *not my fault*."

Rafe grinned above her, and settled warmly upon her, his cheek next to hers. "I've got you where I want you, little miss goddess of the harvest," he whispered in a pleased, amused and teasing tone.

She wiggled her hips, adjusting for the deeper fit, and smoothed the rapidly beating pulse in his throat. "I find this very fulfilling."

He eased deeper and she gasped. "Very fulfilling," Rafe noted and bent to capture her breast in his mouth.

"You're playing with me," she whispered unevenly when she could speak. "You're playing with me and we're making love at the same time."

"We're adjusting to each other, sweetheart. You could play with me."

"I like this. Is it always like this?" she asked desperately, fearing that she was dreaming. "Of course, it isn't, I remember—"

Rafe's hand skimmed slowly downward and came between them, touching her delicately in exactly the right spot. She arched, struck by the impact of riveting waves of pleasure. Moments later, she blinked. "I bit your shoulder. *I bit your shoulder*," she repeated horrified. "Rafe, every word is true in that article—I actually, oh, please, please don't be embarrassed—I actually cried out."

He nuzzled her breasts and gathered her tighter beneath him, one hand lifting her hips to him. "Demi, don't...just don't be too shocked. Don't think too much about your articles and don't analyze the situation. We're doing nicely."

She smoothed his rippling back, caressed it. "Yes, of course. We're equating. Lovely equation. You know why I'm furious with Thomas, don't you?"

He stiffened. "Could you leave Thomas out of this?"

"I'm glad you've come to me, Rafe. I'm glad you—we're here now and that we are intimate." She flicked her tongue into his ear and Rafe let out a hard taut groan, stiffening above her. With his hair peaked from her fingers, he looked rumpled, fierce and delicious.

She licked her lips, moistening them for the attack she planned on his mouth. She tightened her body around his and watched his features harden grimly. "Demi—" Rafe's deep voice shook. His whole body shook.

She loved the feeling of power, as if she, who always put others first was riding a dangerous cliff, taking what she wanted. Dear Rafe, her friend, her gentle, caring— She flung her arms around him and let him take her into the heat, his body flying with hers, the rhythm pounding against her soul, making her so happy she could laugh.

Instead her cry came high and keening into the night stars, as if she'd given a part of herself to Rafe.

The pounding storm ran on, pouring from his body to hers, or were they one now? Rafe stiffened, his expression taut, his eyes locking with hers, his strong hands pinning hers, fingers laced.

He came softly down to her, this wonderful man, trusting her to take care of him, to soothe the primitive, slowing rhythm of his heart.

"Did I hurt you?" he asked unevenly, his lips tender against her throat.

Demi searched through the riveting heat wave that had just tossed her body up on some golden plane and the feathers that had carried her gently down to reality. She ran her hand across his chest, tested the slowing beat of his heart, and whispered, "I am stunned, yet... No, you gave me delight, not pain."

Rafe's breathing stopped. "I didn't hurt you. You're all right," he stated again, as if reaffirming the thought in his mind. "Did you say 'delight'?" he asked slowly and then began to laugh, pleasing her for some unknown reason.

"What do you mean, you never made love to your wife?" Demi stared at Rafe, who stood, legs braced apart looking up at the small cliff they would scale. The wind riffled his hair, and she latched her hand on the back pocket of his cutoffs, letting her gaze drift lower to his beautiful, taut, muscular legs, flecked with hair.

He crouched to check the laces on her climbing boots, tightening them, and his hand stayed to slide up her bare inner thigh. One finger slid teasingly inside her shorts, one of many caresses he had given her since their lovemaking last night. Though he had refused to make love again, fearing it would hurt her, Rafe had gently pleased her. One touch had taken her shivering into delicate contractions and Demi had shocked herself. According to the articles, she could possibly—accidentally—be a responsive, sensual woman.

That woman couldn't believe that Rafe didn't make love to his wife. Demi reached out with both fists and grabbed his sweatshirt, drawing him down to her. "You mean you never made love to your wife, and...does that mean that you are only a one-timer?" she demanded, fearing that she would never experience his beautiful body again. "I understand Madeline's desperation for you. Perhaps you should have told her that you do not repeat performances."

Rafe looked pained and gently tugged her fists away, bringing her palms to his lips. "I wish you wouldn't do that. No, I never made love to Sara Jane. We were like brother and sister."

"What about Madeline? What was your relationship with her?" She watched fascinated as Rafe glared at her.

He tied the line running from his waist to the loops on her belt. "Madeline and I—never mind. Sara Jane gave me something when I needed it. I like to think that I helped her through a rough patch."

"People don't get married for that reason, Rafe."

"Oh? Why did you get married?"

Demi understood that Rafe wanted to protect himself, that he didn't like admitting how noble and good he was. Somehow his dark code of honor allowed for a steel heart and balked at tenderness. "I wanted to take care of Thomas. He reminded me of my father. I understood him, his needs and it seemed a good

match. I was ready to get married and we liked the same literature.''

Rafe's emerald green gaze pinned her. ''What about your
needs, Demi? Have you thought about them?''

She had plenty of needs: raw ones, ones that involved spreading
Rafe beneath her and having her way with his lovely body. His
look at her sizzled and held. She shivered and feared that he
couldn't be attracted to her, that their lovemaking last night had
never happened. ''You're not thinking of taking my castle again,
are you? When you came, you wanted to know what I wanted. I
wanted to save my father's dream and I think I have. I don't think
I understand your relationship with Madeline. Oh, my. You had
an affair with her while you were married to Sara Jane, didn't
you?''

Rafe scowled down at her briefly, turned and began climbing
up the cliff. He turned and looked over his shoulder to her. ''You
are the only woman in my experience who has the ability to—
No, I did not have an affair with Madeline while I was married.
I knew it would hurt Sara Jane.''

''Well, what about this love affair business?'' she called up to
him and admired the way his muscles rippled and bunched as he
worked his way upward. ''Do you intend to marry her? Madeline
would make an excellent corporate wife, you know, business din-
ners, society wives' clubs, supporting the husbands—''

Rafe's smile down at her was chilling. ''Don't try to organize
my life for me. Okay, sweetheart?''

''I know about wives supporting husbands in business—''

''Lay off.''

A half hour later, Demi stepped onto the rock and Rafe's hand
tugged her to safety. She laughed, delighted with the triumph of
the short climb, following his careful instructions, pitting herself
against a task. She stood on tiptoe to kiss Rafe briefly. ''You've
given me a wonderful gift. Without you, I would never have—''

He stood back from her, winding the rope between them, drawing her closer. His hands smoothed her waist, and she knew from

his dark look that he wanted her. He turned her slowly and stood with her in his arms. "Look."

The valley spread out before them, the small castle looking complete near the lush green meadow. "The cows look so tiny. I see your brother's helicopter."

Rafe's hands tightened on her waist, then freed her. "He's not my brother. We're half brothers. Nick and Joel don't know it."

Demi turned to him. The pain clouding his face terrified her. She sensed instantly that this was the dark shroud enfolding Rafe, a secret that tore at him, that could devour him. She had to protect him. Demi grabbed his sweatshirt in her fists. "What do you mean?"

His painful expression deepened as he eased his chest back, tugging her hands away. He rubbed his chest. "We're not full brothers. We had the same father, but not the same mother. I just discovered that a week before meeting you. Nick and Joel are real brothers. I'm not. I don't know who my mother is."

She shook her head. "I don't understand. How can Nick and Joel not know? Don't you want to know about your real mother?"

Rafe leaned back against the sun-warmed rock; he plucked a stalk of scrub grass embedded in a crack and twirled it in his fingers. He wanted to let Demi know what he was, what kind of people he came from. But he only knew his father's family and the memories weren't pleasant.

He watched a doe cross the meadow below, moving into the sumac bushes. "My father raped a fourteen-year-old girl. Belinda—Joel and Nick's mother—arranged to take the baby. Belinda padded herself and my father was busy with other women and his schemes, and she simply presented him with another baby when he turned up. When she knew she was dying, just six months after Nick's birth, she left a letter with a friend. That friend recently found it when she was cleaning out their safe-deposit box and sent it to me. Belinda wanted me to know everything, because she thought I might one day want to meet my real mother and because she wanted me to know that she loved me as if I were her own son. Nick and Joel don't know," he repeated, struck once more by how apart he was from brothers who united, had survived.

He glanced at Demi—sweet, warm, compassionate, innocent—looking as though she wanted to leap into his past and smooth it into the picture-perfect, all-American boy's life. He didn't want to hurt her, bringing her into his pain, his past. Rafe stared out into the mountains, red rock jutting upward out of the snow, leaving the lush timber below, like realities cutting through dreams. He shrugged. "End of story."

"I think it's beautiful. Belinda loved you terribly and she helped a frightened girl, too young to deal with a child," she whispered. She stroked his jaw, turning him to her. "I hate it when you look so lonely, and now I know why. Thank you, Rafe, for giving me a part of you."

"Beautiful?" Images of Lloyd's cruelty slid through Rafe, the hardships he and his brothers endured, the way his older brother, Joel, fought to keep them fed and warm. "Beautiful isn't the word. Lloyd killed the Tallchiefs' parents during a convenience store robbery. Fiona ran us off from the funeral. I don't blame her."

"You—the sons of the murderer—tried to come to the Tallchiefs' funeral?"

Rafe slashed his fingers through his hair. "It was a stupid idea. But we were teens, living on the streets and wanting to change. We had this big dream of Palladin pride—" Rafe inhaled abruptly, remembering how much they wanted to have honest lives, homes, and how much they ached for a family. "We were headed for nowhere, with juvenile records. When Mamie came around, Lloyd propped us up, dressed us in clean clothes. We knew we'd better lie and appear happy. She never knew how bad it was. She still doesn't."

"Rafe—" Demi's eyes were huge, filled with tears, her hand soft upon his cheek.

"Lay off. I don't need your sympathy." Damn, he wanted to

hold her. His heart was shredded by pain. Instead the old protective instincts had surged into the clean mountain air, reminding him that he was bred to hurt, to abuse; he had a dark legacy that would always hurt tender hearts.

"I wasn't going to give you sympathy. I still think it's a beautiful story." Tears glistened on her lashes and unable to bear the pain, Rafe stood and flicked the rope, preparing to climb again.

Because he'd hurt her, struck out at her in his pain, Rafe decided to throw his whole unsavory life at Demi. She'd see him as he really was—Lloyd Palladin's bastard son. Rafe turned, hooked his thumbs in his pockets and braced his boot upon the hard rock as the past slammed against him. "You have a heritage, descended from Tallchief and Una, the romance of Elizabeth and Liam. I have nothing. I believe in reality, not dreams and when I want something, I usually take it. Do you think that I'd come after you like Liam came after Elizabeth, offering your father trade beads and sheep and land for you? Do you think I'd actually take time to—make gifts for you, like Liam's beaded moccasins for Elizabeth? That I'd actually spend my time on something so frivolous? Oh, yes, I study my potential acquisitions and I read Elizabeth's letters in your father's study. Don't imagine for one minute that I'm a gentleman, or romantic. Liam and Tallchief are your heritage, not mine. I'm in the business of profit, Demi, and good at it. I'm quick, neat and ruthless."

He watched her reel backward as though she'd taken a blow. Rafe shot out a hand and pushed her safely against the jutting rock. "You might as well know. When my father spotted this castle and developed his scheme to sell that money pit to some unsuspecting buyer...we helped—Joel, Nick and I. We came here as boys, worked to hide the rot and crumbling block. We killed rats so big—"

He didn't want to frighten her. "It took years before someone trusting enough came along. I was a part of your father's losing his retirement and his health. He should have it back and you shouldn't have to work so hard. Palladin, Inc.'s offer to buy the castle stands, anytime you decide you'd like it. You're attached to the castle, so I'm certain we could work details."

Then he turned, lifted his eyes to the scrub pine branches swaying overhead and the dark green fringes against the clean blue sky. Rafe tried to wipe away the image of Demi, her eyes wide and shocked, her hand covering her lips, her wild, pained cry shooting into the clear mountain air. "Rafe!"

He stiffened, braced against his pain and inhaled the cold mountain air unsteadily. A chipmunk leaped across the rocks, reminding him of Demi, rushing to save the people she loved. He turned to see her face pale in the bright sunshine, her braids, spilling over her shoulders like woven silk. Rafe tightened his body against the new surge of bitterness and self-disgust. He was his father's son, taking advantage of a woman who was no more than a girl—whose only flaw was in caring for others so much that she had forgotten herself. She'd been hurt by one man, betrayed, and now Rafe had finished the job.

It was better that she had no illusions about him; Rafe didn't deserve them. Rafe wanted Demi to know the whole truth, tossing it out into the clear, fresh air. "You might as well know, Miss Tallchief, that we're not exactly roughing it, pitting ourselves against the wilderness. Down sleeping bags and camping gear aren't thin blankets and coffee can rabbit stew that my brothers and I shared. I did not plan this little camping trip to please you entirely. My motives were selfish. I knew what would appeal to you and I wanted to seduce you. I wanted to take that lush, sweet body and to claim it for myself. We're going to the cave, and back to camp where you will pack your things. We're leaving at first light."

Demi stepped into the small cave, high on the mountain, almost hidden by scrub brush. The afternoon sunlight shot into the cave, sending the crystals' myriad of color and light out to greet her. Clusters of crystals clung to the rocks as if they had waited for years for her, just for her. Demi spread her hands in front of her, watching the colors dance across her skin and thinking of Elizabeth, who had written, *I had already given him my body and his son, and now, I gave him my love.*

Rafe stepped into the cave beside Demi, expertly scanned the rock floor and the sides of the shallow, tiny cave for danger.

"It's beautiful." Demi touched a crystal cluster, running her fingertip across the multifaceted points. "Look at the beautiful colors."

She turned to Rafe, who was watching her. Bands of light touched his face, lighting his eyes to emerald.

He'd given her more than he knew, giving her a piece of his life, hidden away in the darkness. He'd told her with his eyes, those beautiful emerald eyes softening to meadow jade, how much he wanted her.

She had to know. "What do you see in the crystals, Rafe?"

He scanned the cave quickly. "Sunlight dancing on silver. Spears of red. Like fire."

"Yes, fire will do nicely." Demi's greed for Rafe shocked her. "I would like you to kiss me, right here, right now."

He scowled down at her, but bent to give her a hard, fast kiss before gently removing a perfect, tiny cluster of crystals. The small crystals shone in her palm, the lights dancing upon Rafe's hard face, spraying into the darkness around him, the colors dancing on his shoulders. He looked as if he were wearing a cloak of sparkling colors. "You're crying," he stated harshly as though he were the reason for her tears.

"I'm crying because of the beauty of the moment. Don't you feel it?" She touched the red dot of color on his lips. "Oh, Rafe, that perfect crystal you gave me with the sketch? You saved that all those years, didn't you? From when you and Joel and Nick came here as boys. It meant something to you and you gave it to me."

"I found it when we were working at the castle, disguising the rot with good boards." He scanned her face, rubbed away a tear with his thumb and shook his head. "Tears should be for the gentle, Demi. Don't expect me to feel or to understand. I can give you nothing—no promises, not the sweet words you deserve.''

Demi clutched the crystals in her palm, just as she wanted to protect Rafe from his dark legacy. ''What do you deserve, Rafe?''

His emerald eyes flashed down at her, the colors dancing around him. Rafe was wary, and ready to wrap his dark shroud around him. ''I have what I want. Don't count on me for husband material, Demi. I'm not a good candidate.''

''Why, Rafe, I thought you knew. I'd never consider you for husband material. I'll never marry again,'' Demi whispered when she could speak. ''Oh, look. There's something tied to that cluster! It's hidden in that tiny niche—''

Rafe reached past her and carefully unknotted leather thongs, holding the leather roll. The thongs crumbled in his fingers. Layers of aged oiled leather reluctantly released the prize: a broken bronze grip of a sword, elaborately encrypted with Celtic designs.

Eight

"**W**hat are you doing?" Rafe asked in an outraged tone as Demi sat on his bedroll and tugged his feet onto her lap. His scent was that of the soap he'd used to bathe in the cold mountain stream, mixed with campfire smoke and leather scents. The evening campfire light flicked over his rugged face, stubble darkening his jaw, making him appear tough and dangerous. With his long jean-clad legs in front of him, and wearing a flannel lined, denim jacket, he looked as Western as the saddle bracing his back.

Demi hugged his feet. He wasn't tough and dangerous, of course. He was thoughtful and sweet, preparing a bucket of hot water for her, and setting aside soap, clean towels and giving her the privacy he thought she needed. She knew how tender he could be, even when he was fighting the past. If he thought that he had terrorized her with the truth about his life, he was mistaken. Sharing his life with her, the hard realities that she doubted he gave to anyone, had only endeared him more to her.

"You just drink that chamomile tea and relax." Demi pulled

Rafe's socks from his feet and ignored his glare, made even more fierce by the firelight stroking the hard angles of his face, the grim lines bracketing his mouth.

"A man's feet are private," he muttered as she held and caressed them. They were large, strong, and his toes wiggled uncomfortably when she touched him, as though they were shy.

"I'm going to give you a relaxing foot massage, and you're going to hold still. Stop squirming and glaring and drink your tea."

Rafe hadn't spoken a word since his declaration in the afternoon. He'd grimly fetched firewood, cooked supper and then had settled down in the firelight to brood. She rubbed his insole with her thumb and ran it across the ball of his foot. He glared at her as she stroked his toes, massaging her new ylang-ylang and sesame oil mixture into them. "What are you trying to prove?"

"That you need to relax. You can't just go shooting arrows at a girl's castle, take her for a lovely camping trip, give her a perfect crystal that is dear to you, find a marvelous Celtic sword grip in the cave and then try to spoil it with your bad mood." She kneaded his foot, using her thumbs to smooth the ball of his foot. She sensed Rafe's tense, wary mood. Demi had to be very careful with him, protecting him from the past and she noted that though he was uncomfortable with her touch, he did not take his feet from her keeping.

She poured more oil into her palms, rubbed them together and then smoothed his long toes, one by one, imagining them stroking hers as she placed her thoughts into a logical line. "I'm glad you brought me here. It's a lovely place and it's unlikely that I would have seen it without you. Father will be thrilled with the sword grip. I'm certain he can read the symbols, once it is cleaned."

"Uh-huh." Rafe looked at her warily as she massaged his ankles, stroking the taut tendon down to his heel. "Don't you get it? I seduced you, Demi. It was my purpose to get you out of that damned, broken-down, cold workhouse and have you to myself. I wanted you."

She shielded her blush with her hair falling loosely along her cheek. "That pleases me," she whispered, smoothing his toes again and running her fingertips in circles around the sole of his foot. "Drink your tea."

"It's herbal. I like coffee and you're off the mark. If I wanted my toes...romanced...I'd pay a masseuse. Why don't you want to get married again?" he shot at her.

Demi massaged his toes carefully, lodging her fingers between them. She studied the fit, wiggling her fingers and Rafe stiffened as though he were uncomfortable. "It isn't right for me. I'm not the only one who works hard. You rarely spare time for yourself and you rarely relax. You like to be difficult."

"Why isn't marriage for you?" Rafe's voice was very quiet.

"Let's not drag out old laundry, shall we?" She cradled his foot within her hands and continued massaging it. She loved touching him, watching him, exploring him and didn't want the unpleasantness of her marriage shadowing the moment.

Rafe's breath seemed to explode from him, as though he had been holding it too long. "Something you learned in one of those articles, I suppose."

"You can bristle all you like, but you're enjoying this."

"Is that so?" Challenge was in his voice, his jaw tightening. "Don't do that...do not do that," he warned as she cradled his feet in her lap and hugged them tightly.

Demi smiled to herself. Rafe wasn't denying that he liked her touch. "You're a good man, Rafe. You have a kind heart. You could have manipulated our creditors and used Palladins' resources to force a sale—directed by your grandmother's wishes—but you didn't. You took time to deal with my father in the gentlest way, persuading him to go to Arizona, and he hasn't a clue it was for his health. You could have exposed my plan at any moment, but you didn't. You've arranged so many wonderful things, like the chicken coop, and helped make my retreat a success. I could have never folded all those brochures the other night without you. Thank you. Now, don't you think it's time you stopped being so hard on yourself? Don't you think it's time to recognize how wonderful you are?''

Rafe placed the tea mug aside, his look at her determined. "Look, Demi, I thought we settled this earlier. I'm not exactly Mr. Nice Guy. It's not in my genes. You can't shove me into the men you usually push around.''

His eyes narrowed. "You know, there are lots of women who consider me as husband material.''

"Hush. Don't start getting tough now. I won't have it. You can act surly all you want with Joel and Nick.''

Rafe grabbed her wrists and tugged her to him, his expression fierce. "Listen, you little fix-it. I won't have you trying to repair my life. It can't be fixed. I can handle myself and I won't have you nurturing me like you do your father and that miserable excuse for an ex-husband. I'm not in the nightshirt social set.''

"Thank you for making me feel as though I appealed to you.''

Rafe frowned blankly. "What do you mean?''

"I know what last night cost you. You seemed absolutely exhausted later. You didn't have the strength to remove yourself—''

"Let me get this straight. Good old Thomas probably removed himself from your bed immediately and you were expecting me to react the same way.''

She couldn't stop the flush moving up her cheeks. "You are a very tender man, Rafe Palladin. The encounter was lovely and not one I'll ever forget—slow, thorough, tender, very warming and surprising. You gave me that.''

"You make me sound like properly aged and barreled wine. Weren't you listening when I told you that I brought you here to seduce you? Doesn't that give a clue that I serve my own needs?'' He inhaled unsteadily, staring at her lips.

She looked down at the buttons of his flannel shirt and the wide red suspenders on his shoulders. She might never have another chance to experience his slow, sure, lovely way of making love. Her heart began to pound heavily, faster, desire skittering along her skin and sinking low in her body. Flashes of last night,

Rafe slowly filling her, pleasing her hurried by, heating her. On impulse, she eased his suspenders off. "Rafe, I fear I have my own needs. I fear I must—"

He seemed fascinated, staring at her bottom lip, which she had just moistened. "Do what?"

Unable to take a stealthy approach, Demi opted for the straightforward. She flung her arms around him and kissed his wonderful mouth with the heat building inside her.

"*Mmmf*—" Rafe went backward, his arms going around her instantly. A button on his shirt tore as she tried to pull it from his jeans. His body jerked as her hand brushed him intimately and Rafe groaned unsteadily.

She looked down at him. She was now the predator, a strong, virile—she corrected the gender—rather, a modern woman who knew what she wanted and was fearless, striking out into her beckoning emotions. A bond ran between them now, heated and strong enough to free her from her fears. Sensuality sprung and pulsed between them like a live, flowing wild heat. He was hers. Her captive and she was greedy for him. "I want you," she whispered unsteadily and noted that his large hand, capable of such great strength, was smoothing her breast gently. "I can't wait."

"Demi—" The protest in Rafe's voice did not stop her. She reached to loosen his jeans and he bolted. "Demi!" This time he sounded shocked.

Demi had a task before her, she couldn't stop. If she stopped— She shimmied out of her jeans and panties and lay upon Rafe, who looked stunned, his hand shakily unfastening his buttons. Uncertain of her own driving emotions, Demi tried to smile an encouragement at him as she unzipped his jeans and pushed up his T-shirt to all that beautiful rippling muscle and skin. "I hope you understand, dear Rafe, but—"

She closed her eyes as she settled upon him and he began to enter her.

She had him. Took him. Devastated him in an unpracticed, hurried, endearing, fluttering, breathless excitement. She pitted herself against him and climbed with him into the heated storm. His rippling muscles, uneven breath and racing heart were hers.

Minutes later, Demi's heart was still racing, her body shivering in the passion that had swept over her, making her throw caution to the night sky.

Beneath her, Rafe looked blankly stunned, as though a mountain thunder and lightning storm had tossed him upon their bedroll. "What was that about?" he asked unsteadily, his hand smoothing her bare hip.

Demi hurried to find reality, racing through her thoughts. "I have no idea. You were here. I was here. I wanted you and I took you. I'm not an impulsive woman. I've never done this before and I'm not certain, but I believe it's called greed. You're not mad, are you? That I took advantage of you? You have every right to be. It was just so lovely the first time and I was looking at you and wondering how your lips would taste, and how you breathed against my skin—just that uneven sound—and how you fitted me perfectly, and how gentle you were, and oh, dear, Rafe...how much I wanted you." She paused for a breath, horrified that she had been so greedy for him, so uncaring and fierce and strong and taking him—

He grinned rakishly. "I liked it, sweetheart."

"'Liked it?' You groaned and shook and tried to dislodge me. I'm very strong. I've never pitted myself against anyone before. I must have terrified you." She blushed furiously against his warm skin, remembering how she had clung to him, locked her body against his and captured him. "Oh, Rafe. I just did Elizabeth's 'Vice Versa.'"

Demi realized that her hair spilled upon him, gleaming and black upon his tanned throat. Rafe looked up at her tenderly, toying with the long strands. He wound one around his thumb and brought it to his lips for a kiss. He grinned slowly, devastatingly. "You did. You really terrified me."

"Good grief, Rafe. Whatever could have come over me? You're shocked, of course. Outraged. Yes, I can understand that—'' Demi struggled to free herself, but Rafe held her tightly, still lodged deeply in her body.

"You're sweet," he whispered, and kissed the tip of her nose. He nibbled on her earlobe and desire slammed into her once more, her body contracting upon his instantly. "Perfect and sweet."

"I'm a savage. I had no idea that I was capable of—" She stared at him, her mind racing— "Rafe, do you realize that this is exactly how Elizabeth must have—must have, you know...Liam? Oh, my. Oh, my. You must hurt terribly. I'm certain a warm pack might help—" She glanced fearfully down and found her expectations to be true—Rafe's jeans were tangled around his ankles. She closed her eyes and shivered. Somewhere in the night, an owl hooted, condemning her. "I am a brute."

"Tell me that you want me again, sweetheart," Rafe whispered when he stopped laughing. He drew her lips down to his. "Sweetheart," he said again, this time more softly as if he meant to memorize the word and use it often, and then he held her very close and tender. Words were not necessary, because Demi sensed that both their hearts were at peace.

Later, Demi settled down close to Rafe with a feeling of coming home. His arms gently, safely enfolded her, his chin settling over her head, nuzzling her. His fingers smoothed her hair, and his hand drew her head close to rest upon his chest. After years of restless, undefined whimsical dreams and placing her needs aside, Demi gave herself to the feeling of being cherished as a woman.

Flashfire! Rafe thought as he looked into Demi's drowsy gray eyes in the predawn light creeping over the mountain. He wanted to wake up with her every morning. He no longer felt isolated and alone, but as though he had bonded to Demi, as though he had changed. Locked in his thoughts, luxuriating in the soft woman in his arms, cuddling her, Rafe had only dozed. After a perfect night of her nude, soft body nudging him in the double sleeping bag, tangling her legs with his and moaning and crying out in her sleep, Demi had begun to awaken.

The whole process of Demi's moods fascinated Rafe, his senses leaping, awakening to the slamming of desire into his body, mixed with the tenderness, which was new and slightly frightening to him. Rafe held very still, waiting for the delight that was Demi to make her first move.

She pressed her cold nose against his shoulder for warmth, nuzzled his skin briefly and sniffed delicately. She moved slightly, nuzzling the hair on his chest. She stroked his chest lightly, her hand finding his hardened nipple. Her fingertips circled it. The unique sensation of being sniffed, stroked and nuzzled again by a woman he desired startled Rafe. Her eyes slowly opened to meet his. He watched, fascinated, as she licked her bottom lip and her drowsy look changed into a hungry tigress, ready to leap upon her prey. Rafe wallowed in the moment when she would make her next move; his body surged to pounding life and he prayed that he was on her menu.

Demi slowly, carelessly arched, stretching her arms high over her head. She yawned, delicately; then she flipped over on him.

Rafe shuddered, her body squirming to accept his hard one immediately. She flung herself into her task, her hips pressing rhythmically upon him, her fevered kisses running across his face. Her long, soft, pleased moans changed tempo, the enchanting melody, unraveling the harsh reality of his life.

Rafe glowed. He knew he was grinning, basking in delight, and couldn't stop. In the next moment, just after he claimed her breast and took it gently to his lips, the tempo leaped, matching the pounding of her heart and of his. The moment her body tightened on his, Rafe lost control, surging upward and pouring himself into her.

"You wilt beautifully," he whispered later to Demi, who sprawled upon him, gently smoothing his chest with brushes of her lips.

"All of it is true...every word in the articles." She sounded stunned.

Rafe kissed the top of her head. He could have held her forever, her soft flesh a part of him, her heart racing against his. "All in the name of research, I suppose."

She shook her head and suckled his nipple experimentally, moving to the other while Rafe wondered if he'd go insane while she played. "Not exactly. I awoke and feared it was all a dream, the way you hold me, the way you breathe as if you can't catch your breath and the heavenly, hungry way you kiss me. There at the end, it wasn't all that sweet, nor gentle. Or I wasn't that gentle. But then, at the moment, I needed to— Oh, Rafe, I needed to take you. I know, I've always been an organizer, a scheduler where men are concerned," she finished breathlessly, desperately.

She turned her hot face against his throat, her lashes fluttering. Her hand flopped upon his chest. "This must be uncomfortable for you. I feel as if my bones have melted. I'd move if I could."

"Let's watch the dawn together, like this, and then I'm going to bathe you," he suggested, smoothing the last shiver from her body over his. After kissing her bare shoulder, he covered it gently and gathered her close to him. At last, Rafe felt complete, the ache gone. He wanted to keep the feeling close, because reality would come too soon.

"I really couldn't let you—bathe me? Oh, no." Her hot face pressed against his neck. "I'd be too embarrassed, but the dawn is lovely," she whispered as the pink light crept higher on the horizon, pushing away the first gray. The birds and chipmunks had begun their chatter.

"Lovely," he repeated and with her cheek next to his, her fingers smoothing the hair on his chest, he wondered when cold reality would tear her away.

"He's down in his office, catching up on work...so he packed you up, and brought you here, did he? My, my, this is a first for him, bringing a woman—not that happy about his methods—to

the family. I put Rafe in his position because he's good at acquiring and product development. I didn't realize he was so traditional,'' Mamie said as she circled Demi slowly, inspecting her.
"You say he didn't give you a choice, that as soon as you returned from camping, he shoved you into his BMW and whisked
you off here?''

"He said he wasn't letting me go, not just yet. I had no
choice...and I am not happy." Demi gripped her hands together
as the small, spry champagne blond woman circled her. She surveyed the penthouse, high in the Palladin, Inc. building. She'd
been plucked from her safe life and tossed into a plush, very
expensive suite, circled by windows that looked out into the Denver skyline. She felt like the tiny fronds on the fern, swaying
gently in the circulating air, delicate and forced to move as others
saw fit. "I do not want to hurt your feelings, but your grandson
kidnapped me. I am not used to being hustled, shoved and having
my life rearranged for me. Because he has been nice to my father,
and...ah...ah...nice to me, I will not press charges. All I want to
do is to get back to my business. It's Thursday now, and I have
students arriving tomorrow evening. I have work to do.''

Awakening in a vast, unfamiliar bed, a maid covering her bare
feet with a satin comforter, had terrified Demi. She'd leaped to
her feet and hurried to find Rafe. Instead she found the older
woman, who introduced herself as Rafe's grandmother, Mamie.
She was dressed in a hot pink leotard and exercise tights. Denver
sunlight skimmed into the spacious, modern room and touched
the woman's short, neat champagne blond hair.

"I see. As I understand it, you're used to having free rein with
the men in your life, doing all of the management of such, and
you usually bear most of the burden. You may find that my grandson likes to call the shots, too." Mamie sat on her exercise cycle,
adjusted her gold-glitter joggers to the pedals, set the timer button
and began cycling. "Rafe has always been pushy. And thorough.
Though I interfere at times, now I depend upon my grandsons to

keep Palladin, Inc. perking along in the profit lane. You're angry, aren't you?''

Demi clenched her fists and faced the older woman who was cycling very quickly. "I wasn't asked. I was told. Look at me. Heavens, I didn't have time to go into the castle to check my message machine. Nick's helicopter landed just as we rode down from the mountain. Rafe tossed the horses' reins to his brother, picked me up and ran with me to the BMW. He seems to enjoy bearing me off at his whim. Though we, ah, he has no reason to feel he has that right. Rafe called my father on the way here, to make certain he didn't worry. *I* worry. I'm a businesswoman with students coming this weekend. I don't have a change of clothing, I haven't had a shampoo and shower and—yes, you're absolutely right, he is pushy. He had no right to carry me in here while I was sleeping. Think of how I must have looked—''

"You looked sweet, all snuggled up close against him, smiling against his chest as you slept. He looked so fierce and possessive, as though nothing could take you away from him. He tucked you in—''

Oh, he had tucked her in several times, into his arms as if he would never let her go.... Demi raised her hand to her throat, fear rising in her. "He actually deposited me in your bedroom as if I were a child. When I speak with him, I will inform him that—''

"He's a man of action, honey, and he's trained to acquire what is a good value. He must think you are special." Mamie shrugged, and used the towel that was draped around her neck to wipe the sweat from her face. She lifted the plastic device attached to her gold belt, punched buttons and said, "Rafe, you brought this girl here without a change of clothing. Take care of it."

Demi crossed her arms. On the drive from Wyoming, Rafe had gently made love to her twice. He'd teased her boyishly, and while she was so fascinated with this new, delightful view of him, he kissed her like a man who knew how to take what he wanted, how to acquire a woman. She frowned—she'd dropped off to sleep immediately both times, meanwhile Rafe was kidnapping her in his BMW, taking her to his Denver lair to meet his grand-mother. "I don't want more of his clothing, or his attention, thank you very much. I want to go back to my castle. I have a business to run—and I need a bath."

Mamie stopped pedaling. Her youthful face suddenly aging with shadows. "I am so sorry that my son took advantage of your family. I cut Lloyd off without a cent and then he really began to go bad. I know what it has cost you."

For the first time, Mamie seemed weighted by her years, her thin shoulders drooping. Demi wanted to ease the older woman's pain and placed her arm around her. "My father wanted the cas-tle. He was thrilled. His dreams have come true."

"That doesn't make what Lloyd did right. I know what Dr. Valerian paid for the castle and it was an absurd price. It's my fault, you know. I made excuses for Lloyd and bought him out of most of his trouble. I was a widow, so busy struggling to build and hold Palladin, Inc. that I'm afraid Lloyd was lost in the shuf-fle. He was my only child. I gave him everything, but myself."

"You can't blame yourself. Nick, Joel and Rafe love you and you've done a fine job with them. Well, except for Rafe's ten-dency to want things his way, of course." Demi thought of the way her father had eagerly cashed in his retirement, sold whatever assets he had, and to help him, she had done likewise. "We have what we want. Rafe doesn't seem to understand that."

Demi couldn't be acquired; she'd given everything once and found despair. Rafe had made love to her as though he cherished her and now she knew the difference. If that changed, she couldn't bear the pain. She couldn't afford another mistake....

"He wouldn't. Rafe has little experience with sentimentality. He's worried about you working too hard and something else is bothering him. It's very deep and troubling and apart from you. You're the first girl he's brought to me, you know. I know that his marriage to Sara Jane wasn't hearts and flowers, but—well, I have an idea why he married her and took care of her and her child. All the Palladins have green eyes and that cleft in their chins from birth. Robbie didn't. His eyes are sky blue. Rafe is giving Robbie up too easily. My grandson is a man who never gives up.''

Rafe had shared a part of life with Demi, that he hadn't given Mamie. Would he tell her of Belinda's letter? Demi thought of the small perfect cluster of crystals that Rafe had placed into her hand. She would remember that moment forever. Would he?

A formally dressed butler hovered near her, his arms filled with boxes. ''Madam?''

''My grandson doesn't know what to do with you, but he knew he'd better not leave you. That's why he's good at acquiring property—he stays on the matter until he gets the job done. It doesn't usually take this long for Rafe to get what he wants and that is why I know that you are special to him. If you want to shower, you can use the guest bathroom—it's filled with our latest acquisition, Fifi Flower Fragrances. I'd suggest you take time for a nice long, relaxing soak—perhaps in the Lime and Love froth— because if your temper gets any higher and you and Rafe tangle...''

She answered the buzzing from the device attached to her waist. ''Mamie, here...Rafe, you're lucky she doesn't kill you. She's got that Tallchief blood, you know, and she's not happy now. Yes, the clothes arrived and she's on her way to freshen up.''

''Give me that,'' Demi demanded, and held out her hand. She ignored the humorous glint in Mamie's eyes and spoke into the plastic device. ''Rafe Palladin, you are in trouble. You can't just—''

She listened to his quiet murmur, an order given and the shuf- fling of papers, the scratch of a pen. ''What was that, sweet- heart?'' he asked in a distracted tone.

''Big deal going down,'' Mamie whispered with a grin. ''He's acquiring a nice piece of property. Nice lush fields, good for cattle or sheep. My grandson always had a feel for the land and what was right. He likes cattle and growing things. That's why he's in charge of our ranch. I always thought he'd have a whole gang of kids to keep me company, in my old age.''

"Rafe?" Demi asked very softly, when she wanted to scream. The pen-scratching-on-paper noise continued. "Uh-huh, sweetheart?"

"I am not happy," she said very firmly and gave the device back to Mamie. The men in her experience knew what to expect when she pronounced unhappiness. They usually obliged and tried to right the situation; she expected the same from Rafe. "I objected to every mile on our way here. I talked until I was exhausted. I tried to run away. I could have him arrested, you know."

The older woman adjusted the pink headband on her forehead. "What did Rafe say?"

"He said I would like you—which I do. And then there were his...methods." Demi turned to shield her blush from Mamie. "He can be very persuasive. I never knew I was ticklish."

Mamie frowned curiously. "Let me get this straight— Rafe...my Rafe, tickled you."

"He did." Demi omitted the way Rafe playfully nuzzled her bare stomach and the delighted squeal that had welled out of her, surprising her.

"Madam?" the butler asked Demi. "Your things are waiting in the bathroom. Might I suggest a lie down before dinner with the Palladins this evening? Would you like anything special? I could change the menu—"

"Anything would be lovely, I'm certain." Demi tried for dignity and hurried to the bathroom. While she was showering in the luxurious room, she would think about how to attack Rafe in the most effective way. Anger was unfamiliar to her and she wasn't certain how she would react to Rafe when she saw him again. A little revenge wouldn't hurt.

Demi decided not to wait, to speak to Rafe without his grandmother's protection. She hurried to shampoo and shower, and dressed quickly in a yellow Palladin, Inc. sweat suit, the least costly of the outfits, which included a simple turquoise evening sheath. After wrapping a towel around her damp hair, Demi hurried out of the penthouse apartment, stepped into a luxurious elevator and waited for the elevator to go down one flight. She stepped off and asked a woman, who was dressed in a business suit and wearing a name tag, to direct her to Rafe Palladin's offices. She ignored the woman's pleas to stop, and raced to devastate the man who had interfered with her life.

Primed to tell Rafe that he was overbearing, too bossy and illogical, Demi burst into his office. Dressed in a three-piece, pin-striped navy business suit with a light blue shirt and diagonally striped tie, Rafe was walking slowly across the room, clipping off a dictation to a beautiful blond woman in a short skirt.

Demi blinked and locked her bare soles on the lush pearl gray carpeting. The woman's legs were endless—she was tall, lithe and perfectly tanned. The suit-clad woman who had been following Demi, begging her to stop, bumped into Demi's backside. The woman sent a pleading look to Rafe. "Mr. Palladin, I am so sorry. I don't know who this person is...she's not wearing a name tag."

"Thank you, Mrs. Davis. I have been expecting her."

Mrs. Davis clutched her clipboard. "But sir, one of Palladin, Inc.'s rules is that all unidentified personnel should be wearing a name tag."

Rafe shot her a narrowed look. "This is Demi Tallchief. See that everyone knows who she is. She is to have free access to any Palladin properties, including this room." Rafe's cool tone said he wasn't arguing. He glanced at Demi, his gaze moving slowly over the towel wrapped around her head, down her yellow sweat suit. When he stared at her bare feet, something hot and wicked and amused flickered in his eyes. They slowly turned to soft meadow jade and rose to study her face. "My grandmother said you'd escaped the penthouse. She seemed to think that you were on the warpath and out to get me. Could that be true? Sit down, Demi."

The blonde at his side speared Demi with an unpleasant glance.

She crossed and uncrossed her lengthy legs, hiking up her short skirt. "Shall I go?"

"We're not done." Rafe glanced at Demi, who had just eased into a chair before her knees failed her. He continued pacing across the room, his dictation in clipped, efficient sentences, laid out like a military campaign. He was just as cold and controlled as when she had first met him. She saw the raw power and determination in Rafe, the man born to take and make lives and fortunes. This man could have easily crushed her efforts to save her father's dream. Demi shivered; this man was not her gentle lover, the boyish tickler of the trip to Denver. Unique tops of all sizes and shapes lined the shelves behind him, resembling soldiers waiting for his command.

Demi wiggled her bare toes on the lush carpeting, very aware of the meticulous, beautiful blond secretary, and of her own shortcomings—a mere five-foot-five height, ample curves, and straight black hair—not a drop of glamour or intrigue in the practical mix. She frowned at Rafe, who had dragged her into a world she hadn't cared enough to read about, to research and prepare. He ripped off his jacket, tossed it onto a long low couch and briskly rolled up his shirtsleeves, glancing at his watch as he dictated. He glanced at Demi again, his eyes narrowed on her bare feet. He frowned, his fist crushing the papers in his hand. "Are you wearing a ring on your toe?"

"I believe I am." The ring was the result of a new article, which dealt with startling lovers and getting attention. Unless Demi misunderstood, she had Rafe's complete attention, or rather the ring on her toe did. "Do you have time to talk with me? I have a slight problem about my schedule being wrecked."

He stood so long, staring at her feet, that Demi moved them beneath the chair.

"Now where was I?" he asked the secretary, who repeated a phrase to remind him, and then he was mapping a campaign to acquire a perfect location for a sporting goods store. He verbally sketched ideas for a fly fishing demonstration, a camper display, tent setups and a huge live fish tank, ideas to be enlarged by the advertising and development team. Demi shifted uneasily. She'd been ignored by men all her life, but Rafe wasn't getting away with it.

Another older woman came into the room, bringing Demi a cup of chamomile tea. Demi recognized her immediately. "You're—"

The secretary patted Demi's shoulder. "Mrs. Jones. You're wonderful. My husband is acting pretty frisky nowadays." She winked and whispered, "He wants me to come back next year."

"Did Mr. Palladin send you?" Demi asked and returned the warning glare Rafe shot at her.

"Yes. I loved it. Will you broaden your seminars to include something for men?" When Demi stared at her, wondering how she could possibly lecture men on sensuality, the woman winked. "I'm trying my Demi's Delites tonight, you know the little lace and rosettes shortie with the ruffled panties? Do you suppose you could start a catalog business?"

"Mrs. Jones, are you quite finished? Perhaps you have work to do?" Rafe invited too softly. When Mrs. Jones left with another wink, Rafe ran his hand through his hair, then leaped into another project and dictated a softly lethal letter to a manager of a shoe store chain. The chain had improperly displayed Palladin's line of women's shoes. Rafe threatened to jerk the franchise; he pivoted and began to pace back across the gray expanse of his office carpet. He punched an intercom button and snapped, "Brush."

Demi locked her fingers to the chair's arms; the single command was probably a code word, a necessary access to a private vault or database storeroom, so precious that it required a password. A powerful man in control of himself and the business before him, Rafe shot a penetrating glance at her. He seemed unapproachable, not at all like the man who had made love to her so desperately in the BMW, parked in a stand of pine trees. This man arranged fortunes, lives and moved the elements in his life to suit him. He seemed to be made of ice and hard steel, each decision spearing directly to the heart of the problem, isolating it and giving a direction to settle it.

Demi frowned at him. *He had taken charge of her life; she couldn't allow that, not when she was learning so much about herself and her needs—now, one of them was revenge.*

"I'm done," he said suddenly, as Nick and Joel entered the room, both dressed in similar business suits. The blond secretary slid another frosty glance at Demi and left quietly, her elegant body swaying. Rafe ignored her, and Demi wondered if he knew how much the woman wanted him.

"Hi, Demi," Nick said as if he saw her in Rafe's office every day. "The castle is safe. I raised the drawbridge. Rafe says this won't take long and then I'll fly back."

"Demi, nice to see you. Rafe, this better not take long," Joel said as he sprawled into one of the chairs bordering a large smooth granite surface set into the plush gray carpeting. "I promised Fiona I'd be home for supper. If Nick can still land a helicopter on a dime, I can just make it."

Nick grinned and sank into a chair next to the granite square. "Married men have time cages. You won't catch me jumping when a woman flutters her lashes."

"Leave this one alone." Rafe moved toward Demi, picked her up and sat, replacing her on his lap. His brothers grinned at her attempt to escape him, which Rafe easily foiled by holding her wrists. He grinned. "Now, Demi, goddess of the harvest, you wouldn't want me to start tickling you again, would you?"

"Rafe, I will—" She realized that she was very new to making threats, but then her father or Thomas had not needed threats as Rafe did.

"Hush. Look," he noted tenderly to his brothers. "She's wearing a toe ring. Isn't that something?"

"Fascinating," Joel murmured with a grin.

"It made my day," Nick added with a matching grin.

Rafe unwound the towel around her head, and smoothed her

hair with his fingers. As if on command, the butler entered the office with a brush and a comb placed on a towel-covered tray. Rafe took the brush and began working it through the ends of her hair, studying it.

Joel and Nick shared an amused look while Demi squirmed. No one took care of her; she had always been in charge. She frowned at him and he tilted her chin, stroking the brush through the hair beside her cheek. He touched the sleek damp strands with his fingertip. "What are you glaring about?"

"I am not a child. No one has brushed my hair since I was a child." Her mother had often been ill and Demi had to learn early how to take care of herself; her father had been too absorbed with research, and his concern for her ailing mother.

"Then it's time someone took care of you. Stop fidgeting."

"Rafe, I—" she began again as Rafe slowly, meticulously brushed her hair. Then he placed the brush aside and drew her close to him, her head beneath his chin.

"I need you here," he said quietly. She held very still, aware that suddenly the silence had grown ominous.

"What's up, Rafe?" Joel asked slowly, stretching out his long legs.

"Okay. Here it is, short and sweet," Rafe said tautly, his arms tightening around Demi. He took a deep breath. "You and Nick are brothers. I am your half brother."

Both men stared at Rafe and beneath Demi, his body tensed.

Demi could have wept for all of them. To protect Rafe, she hurled her arms around him, and kissed his cheek. He softly kissed her lips. She turned hurriedly to his brothers, who looked stunned and confused. "He loves you. He's worried how to tell you, how to make it easier and it shouldn't change how you feel about each other, how you all stayed together and fought for your pride, and—and he wanted you all here together, with Mamie, like the family you are. Together."

Rafe spoke softly. "I'm sorry, Joel. Nick."

"Details," Joel, the attorney, demanded, and Demi held Rafe

tighter, burying her face against his throat as he explained. When he finished, Rafe looked worn and hard, his shadowed look at her ridden with pain.

Demi ached for all of them and slid her fingers between Rafe's. "You can't let this change anything. You've come too far. Look how you've survived. Look how Mamie adores you."

Nick rose to select four tops from the shelves. He tossed one to Joel, gave one to Demi and another to Rafe. He wound the string around his and shot it to the smooth surface between the chairs. "Do we tell Mamie? This could be hard on her. It's one more thing."

Rafe's top hit the smooth surface and then Joel's. "I think it is Rafe's decision. It doesn't change my feelings toward my brother, but Mamie is a different consideration," Joel said quietly as the three tops circled each other. "She may want to know about Rafe's mother. She may want to meet her."

"What do you think, Demi?" Rafe asked as he placed a kiss into her palm and showed her how to wind the string around the beautiful fuchsia splashed top. "Here. Trust me."

"I'm not very athletic." Demi did not want to spoil the brothers' obviously familiar bonding ritual.

"You'll do." He fitted his hand around hers and after a quick movement, the top flipped to the surface and began spinning perfectly. "I knew it. She's a natural."

Delighted that she hadn't failed Rafe, Demi looked at the brothers, obviously loving each other. She looked at the tops spinning on the floor and then at Rafe, who looked as if his heart was tearing. She smoothed the line between his brows and rested her hand along his jaw, petting him. "Everything will work out."

She took her time winding the cord around the top, placing her thoughts as precisely as the cord; then she casually mentioned a nagging thought. "Rafe, you have a lovely secretary. The one who took your dictation?"

She hurled the top onto the surface and waited, her mouth dry while he answered.

Rafe's gaze followed the top while his fingers caressed the back of her neck. "I hadn't noticed. She's someone from the secretarial pool. Mrs. Jones needed a break. She seems distracted at times and she's started blushing. Look at that, Nick...Joel. See that? She's a natural with tops, isn't she?"

The pride in his voice startled Demi. When she looked at Nick and Joel, their hard expressions had eased as they studied Rafe. She loved them all; they were hers to tend.

Nine

Rafe's left eyelid twitched as he towered over Demi. The kitten in his arms hissed at the huge pups, Prince and King, bounding down the stairs. Demi had adopted the orphaned, starving pups and now they were healthy and running to him for a treat. Rafe pointed a finger at them. "Stay."

They plopped to the floor, tongues hanging out while the kitten Rafe had chosen for Demi hissed at them. Rafe placed the kitten into the carrier cage on the table. He had to settle the matter at hand. The kitten reached out to scratch him, reminding him of the furious woman, who had just refused his practical gifts. He plopped the bouquet of wildflowers he had stopped to pick for Demi on top of the carrier cage. "Sweetheart, you shouldn't have sent those appliances back."

On the Monday morning after a successful round of classes and two weeks after her introduction to Mamie, Demi refused to be intimidated by one Rafe Palladin. Mr. Tired Bad Mood had just arrived from Denver. While she adored the flowers he hadn't yet presented to her, the hissing kitten in his arms reminded her of her unsettled, fierce emotions. She continued sweeping the main hall floor. "I could not afford the new deep freezer, the new washer and dryer and the new refrigerator. Not just yet. When my finances will allow, I will purchase them. You should not have ordered them delivered."

The dinner with Mamie had upset Demi. It had the distinct markings of Rafe introducing his intended bride to the family. Demi's experience at being a bride was unsatisfactory.

A dynamic man, the head of Palladin's acquisitions and product development, had caused her to realize that she was a woman with needs. One need was to experiment with her powers as a desirable woman with said acquisitions chief—Rafe acted stunned when she had first tried her hand-feeding-male experiment. Though he held very still, the light burning beneath his lashes told her that she had performed adequately. However, she could not let herself be acquired. Not just yet.

Rafe scowled at her, tossed his briefcase onto the main hall's long table and tore off his suit jacket. He ripped away his tie, tossing it upon the folded layers of Demi's Delites and flicked open his shirt buttons. He rolled back his shirtsleeves in brisk movements that said he was about to tackle a task in which he intended to win. "We're about to have a king-size argument...sweetheart, my goddess of the harvest."

"I never argue. No need." Demi hurried by him, on her way to the kitchen; Prince and King followed her, hoping for food. She couldn't get trapped in marriage again. Not when she had built something for herself. True, The Women's Sensuality Retreat was saving the castle, but Demi felt a sense of accomplishment—something she wanted, worked for and got. Attachment to another man could spoil her magnificent freedom.

While she loved the hissing kitten, all soft and gray and furious, she had to handle the man who was interfering with her life.

Rafe opened the door for her, and his hand flattened on the back of her waist. She caught his unique scent and realized that he intimidated her as her father and Thomas never could. It wasn't fear of Rafe, rather the terror of her emerging, vivid feelings for him. She'd never experienced jealousy before, or the need to compete with a woman, yet Rafe's blond, gorgeous secretary had changed that. Demi struggled with her thoughts, then with determination, placed them aside. She was past dreaming of joined hearts and eternal bonds, and—and children. She'd tossed those dreams upon Thomas, hoping that true love would eventually—

She suspected she loved Rafe and it terrified her. Elizabeth had left a legend in the hollow sword hilt and it applied to Rafe! *'Twil be the knight who brings his lady to this cave with clusters of crystals about—aye, the sparkling crystals shall shoot their cloak of colors about him, who loves her already. Rogue that he is, the lady will love with all her heart.*

"'Tis a new legend, the gift of one woman to another," Elizabeth had written. "My own, dear sweet Liam, the rogue, wore the cloak, colors dancing about him, and I knew I could never deny my love for him, a man of Sioux and Scots blood. Aye, Tallchief and his Una, gave me man—not some easily managed boy, for I am a fierce woman myself. I knew when I rode upon him that I would have his child and the bonds between us would grow. But when he brought me here, to this cave, the lights and colors dancing about him, I gave a new legend to a new land, and to Liam, I gave my heart. Elizabeth Montclair Tallchief."

The colors had danced over Rafe, shimmering around him like a cloak. The legend couldn't be true; he couldn't love her.

Demi turned to Rafe, fighting her emotions. "I wish you wouldn't open doors and place your hand on the small of my back, guiding me through as if I couldn't navigate. All that chair moving, standing for me when I enter a room, and…we're just not compatible, Mr. Palladin. I suggest you leave my castle."

Rafe braced his legs apart, his hands on his waist. "Let me get this straight. You're mad because I took you to meet Mamie, right? That was over two weeks ago and you haven't said a word about it."

She eyed him; he was definitely prepared to battle. So was she. Usually she planned her campaigns, but handling Rafe required head-on confrontation. "You kidnapped me, Rafe. It is different from a nice little date at the local ice-cream parlor, or a little stroll in the woods picking wildflowers. You've been making decisions for me and I'm afraid that will have to stop. Do you know that I haven't given you one gift? And you've given so many?"

"I wouldn't say that." His eyes narrowed, gunslinger fashion. "You like to call the shots. I'm here and I'm calling them when it comes to this. You need those appliances. You should have help—a cook and someone to clean. You've got shadows under your eyes—"

"No, thank you very much. I cannot afford personnel." Demi fought her rising temper; she tried to remember that she had never had a full-blown argument before.

"You muttered," he noted, following her into her bedroom. He pushed open the door she tried to close upon him. He filled up the room just as he filled her thoughts and, frightened of her emotions, Demi ducked under his arm—he looked too starkly, vibrantly male among Demi's Delites silken colors, draped around the room. She hurried out to the kitchen and out onto the lowered drawbridge into the May air. Prince and King bounded happily after her.

"I never mutter. I think I'll plant my herbs just over there, by the drawbridge, giving a little color to the stone and wood. That wall of tumbleweeds should be easy to remove."

While he focused on Demi, Rafe absently scratched Prince's and King's heads. "That's right, run from me. We are having an argument now and you are running away."

"Me run from you? Never. Life was so simple before you decided to acquire the castle. I do hope that idea is not still roaming around your brain."

His eyelid twitched. "I want you to have the damned appliances, Demi."

Prince's and King's ears lifted, their heads cocked to one side as they sensed storms between the humans they loved.

"I couldn't take anything so expensive. If the kitten is for the castle, she's lovely. Thank you." She sniffed, lifting her gaze to meet his. She eyed the man who was raising emotions she had never allowed before, like revenge, anger, hostility, jealousy. She frowned when she thought of his sleek blond secretary, motors running and waiting for him. "One does not always get one's desire, Mr. Palladin."

"I'm getting what I want." The words dropped like concrete blocks into the meadow.

Demi hurried to the cows. They had such understanding eyes. Rafe shot two words out into the sunshine and Demi stopped, her temper riding her. She turned to him. "What was that you said? 'Compulsive female'? I'm compulsive? Just exactly how?"

She glanced down at his polished shoes in the wet lush grass. "You really shouldn't wear those out here."

"You can't push me around, Demi. You're not my mother or my aunt or my sister. Don't offer to polish my shoes or bring me boots. We can't work through this, if you act like my caretaker. I want you as my woman. The balance of the relationship is entirely different. That means I get to take care of you."

I want you as my woman. Demi forced herself to breathe; Rafe's words had stunned her. She petted the cow, Elise, and raced through her thoughts. Discovering her own sensuality and Elizabeth's note that had been hidden in the sword hilt for years had unnerved her. She wanted time to consider the legend, and adapt to the new woman emerging in her—one that wanted Rafe and everything that love entailed. One with her own dreams, not those of other people. Her need for Rafe—ill-tempered as he was now—overrode her desire to please anyone else, including him.

She felt as if she were clinging by her fingertips to a very thin root on a high cliff top and about to sink into a churning, wild mountain river, which could carry her away.

The legend couldn't be true; Rafe couldn't love her.

She couldn't love him.

But there it was—stark, humming, heating, flowing between them—a mix of tenderness, desire, the need to give and take and enough passion riding her to— Everything she'd craved to feel for Thomas was here, now, with Rafe, a man who was her opposite. Life would not flow easily with Rafe.

Love. The revelation was shocking; so was the need to yell at him. Demi reached for a fistful of his shirt, watched that strange wince of pain and let him ease her hand from him. "I wanted to be an intergalactic princess, Rafe," she said, reining the humming anger within her, to a hushed, desperate whisper.

"Why are you whispering?" he whispered back in the meadow filled with sunlight dancing on new grass. Prince and King leaned against his legs as if seeking assurance in emotional storms. He traced a fingertip around Demi's ear, smoothing a strand that had come loose in her quivering anger. "I love the pups, sweetheart, but they're really not included in what is happening between us. Prince. King. Go back to the house."

The pups whined and reluctantly followed Rafe's pointed finger.

"I don't think you heard me, or you'd be laughing." She took a deep breath and yelled, "I wanted to be an intergalactic princess!" She shivered with the rage flowing through her and watched a covey of quail surge into the air. Rafe had done that, stirring her into a bird frightener. She turned to him and unleashed her thoughts in rapid-fire. "Until lately, I forgot that as a child, I wanted to conquer new worlds. But now I remember. My mother wanted me to forget about conquering space and get a practical occupation, one that I could use wherever I went—wherever our family went. After years of transferring universities with Father, she had taken many jobs to help with finances."

"So you just took over her job and transferred that to your ex-husband."

She swallowed, shivered and forced herself to continue, while Rafe swept both hands through his hair. He looked as though he were lost on a twisted path, without an idea how to get to X marks the spot. That exquisite tenderness only for him cruised gently through Demi. She wanted to hold him and soothe him. "You need a haircut. I could do that for you—"

"Demi!" he rasped impatiently.

She stared at her tall, glowering knight, her wake-up call to what *she* really wanted. There in the meadow filled with cows, calves and sunshine, she was angry with herself for all the years lost in others' dreams.

She glared at Rafe. He had caused her to know the difference between a man slaking his momentary needs and a man who enjoyed the feel of a woman, who responded to her touch in a slow, gentle and careful way. Rafe had been extremely gentle with her. Though she knew his fears ran deep to the thought that he would be like his father, Demi was ready to step off into the well of her sensuality and her needs as a woman. Rafe hadn't even noticed her new skimpy black dress before he started yelling at her about returning the appliances.

In the heartbeats while they locked gazes, Rafe rubbed the back of his neck and eyed her warily as if trying to get a fix on her emotions.

Demi rubbed her hands over her face. "I can't afford another—"

"Another?"

"Mistake," she managed to say after a moment of searching for the right word. "You have your pride and I must have mine."

Rafe took a full minute to survey the meadow and the rugged mountains—a muscle contracted and released in his cheek—and then he looked down at Demi. "Let me get this straight. I'm a mistake."

"I'm afraid that I'm using you. You know that you are a very passive, if gentle lover, and there won't be any more of that." Demi shivered, her body wanting his now, humming with the need to kiss his beautiful mouth. *Oh, dear, she mourned. She*

loved him and it terrified her. An avalanche of emotions was
taking her too quickly, before she resolved—

"I am a passive lover, am I? And we're not making love
again?" His tone sounded like hammer hitting steel. "You've
made this decision by yourself and you're expecting to push me
right on down the pansy path you want me to follow, is that
right?"

The meadow shimmered around them, sunlight quivering on
dew, like the emotions running high and terrifying within Demi.
"You have no obligation. We're both adults. Don't snort. You
know I can't determine anything from that sound. Don't think
that I'm a martyr, sacrificing myself, my dreams for my parents.
I love them and they needed me, but that time is past. Now—"

Oh, dear sweet Elizabeth. I can't love him. Love is a prison—

"And now?" Rafe prodded ruthlessly, his tone matched the
rumbling ominous thunder of the approaching storm.

While Demi struggled for an answer, Rafe jerked her to him,
lifting her until her fireman's boots dangled above the meadow.
The raw power should have frightened her; it didn't. She felt safe
and cherished. His eyes burned into hers; his body tense and
trembling. "Lady, I am anything but passive around you."

He cupped the back of her head, slanted and fused his mouth
to hers and kissed her hungrily, hard and spared her nothing.
Caught unaware, Demi's instincts kicked in—she reached for
what she wanted, held him tightly and dived into the heat and
fire. She was shaking, flying, heating, her hands sliding down his
shirt, pulling the buttons free to run through the warm, rough
surface.

Rafe lifted her higher, supporting her bottom and Demi flung
herself more tightly around him, capturing him with arms and
legs and—

Rafe turned slowly in the meadow, his kisses gentling and finally his lips drew away. He breathed unevenly, a vein throbbing
in his throat, and there was nothing gentle about the flickering

depths of his eyes. "Don't push me, Demi. It really wouldn't be wise right now. There is nothing I'd like better than to take you in this meadow, right here in the sunlight, so you'll know exactly how I feel."

Demi shook with the need to have him. Her lips burned, slightly swollen, her neck tingling from his tiny bites upon it, and inside, inside she felt very...hot. She slowly forced her lids to open; she fought for breath. "That was—"

"Savage? Primitive? Well, Miss Tallchief, goddess of the harvest. That is how I feel and after all, I am Lloyd Palladin's bastard son. That is my heritage, not the Tallchief legends." His heart raced beneath her hands, the heat in his eyes burning her.

"You felt all that? Primitive? With me?" she asked incredulously as Rafe slowly turned her again, the sunlight catching the meadow green of his eyes.

He kissed the fingertip she had placed on the cleft of his chin. "I wasn't expecting it. I don't like it. It doesn't fit with the life I want. But there it is. I'll adjust. We'll adjust together. It's called a relationship. I feel very possessive and I want you to feel the same about me. Ridiculous, isn't it?"

His hand caressed her brief clad bottom and he groaned. "Don't tell me. It's that blasted black scrap you made and hung in the bathroom, sizes 8 to 24."

Then he lowered her to the meadow and walked away.

Demi's soft "Rafe, please don't go," caught him midstride. He had to leave before he hurt her, before he let her see how much he wanted her. If he made love to her the way he wanted, letting all that deep passionate heat escape his keeping, Demi could be hurt. His need to take her was savage, driving, conflicting his need to be gentle. Even now, he ached to hold her, to gather her close to him as if she were a part of him. He closed his eyes. Demi had given him so much, and his dark legacy could shatter her at any moment.

His fists ached, curled tightly at his sides. Palladins weren't gentle and Demi could get hurt.

Then there was his heart's hurt-factor. The icy knife lodged in his heart twisted. She didn't want him.

"Rafe?" Demi stood before him, her expression concerned as she looked up at him; her fingertips resting on his chest tethered him more effectively than rope. "I'm sorry I yelled at you."

"Is that what you think this is about? You yelled? Answer me—do you still think I'm after your castle?" Rafe ached while he waited for Demi's answer. Did she trust him? Suddenly he *needed* her trust, and once again he realized how fragile he was with Demi.

She placed her hands along his jaw, her gray eyes soft upon him. "No, I think you're after something else. You frightened me badly. Because I wanted you so fiercely, as if the universe could spin out of control and nothing would matter so long as I was in your arms. You've been so pliable—so gentle that—"

"I hurt you just then." He couldn't bear to look at her lips, the slight red patches where his rougher skin had chafed hers.

"I think I must have hurt you, too. You see, dear sir, I believe you are my...my wake-up call."

"'Dear Sir'?" The business letter language was not an endearment. Rafe realized he badly needed a "darling" or a "sweetheart" tag from her.

Demi leaned against him, snuggled her cheek against his chest and her arms enclosed his waist. "You are very dear. But I'm afraid you've unlocked my rather unsteady emotions. I feel as if I'm coming out of a fog and I'm not certain who I am just yet. If I—if I come to you without understanding who I am, I'll always wonder."

"You're an independent woman whom I admire." Rafe wanted to say more—that he adored her, reveled in her touch and the urge to have a child with her was illogical. He hadn't wanted children, passing on Lloyd's legacy, but now the need surged within him. He feared frightening her. He forced a swallow down his dry throat, and carefully eased his arms around her, nuzzling her hair with his chin. Rafe could have stood forever in the clear bright May sunshine, holding her. "What do you want from me, Demi?"

He'd never felt more vulnerable, and unable to protect himself.

"I want time to understand myself and what is happening between us. Oh, Rafe, please don't ever walk away from me like that again. I felt as if a part of me had been torn away."

"Then, I suppose you could say that I am sometimes in your thoughts?" he prodded, needing that shred of his pride.

"Almost every moment," Demi whispered desperately. "I'm not certain what to do about it. This is all so fast, and I must resolve who I am."

Rafe lifted her chin with the tip of his finger, fell into the soft shimmering depths of her eyes, kissed the single tear on her cheek and knew that he'd give his soul for her. This time, he kissed her with all the tenderness claiming his heart, with all his hopes and dreams for a future with her.

"Father seems so recovered, doesn't he? The visit to Aunt Nell's was good for him. It's only June and with July and August, all warm months ahead of him, he'll become even stronger before winter. Perhaps I can persuade him to visit Nell's during the winter, though the improvements to the castle make it so much warmer. He's quite enthusiastic about my success," Demi said as she bent to crawl into the tepee she had been constructing in the meadow. It leaned dangerously, improperly braced with poles Demi had dragged from the woods. "Rafe, come in. I've been working on this design. I think it will make a unique addition to my classes."

Rafe, dressed in his dress shirt and suit slacks, forced himself not to place his hands on Demi's rounded hips. He'd been so desperate to see her that he'd forced a business conference on Sunday afternoon and had driven all night to get to her. He realized he was sweating; the urge to have her running through him like hot steel. If he could just survive her woman-discovery passages, especially the flirtation ones, he might be more logical.

For a man whose entire life was based on trimming to basics, acquiring what he wanted without wasting time, Rafe had decided to apply old-fashioned courting techniques to Demi. It was too much to ask her to love him, but he thought he had enough love for both of them. Joel was proof that the sons of Lloyd Palladin could love, for Joel's love of Fiona shone deeper every day.

Demi's hips wiggled in her new tight jeans and Rafe wanted to have her in the open meadow. Nathaniel didn't seem to notice that Rafe was courting his daughter. He was much stronger, and once Rafe showed him how to use an ax, Nathaniel enjoyed pitting himself against the wood. Nathaniel frequently spoke affectionately of B. J. Boyd, Nell's reclusive friend.

Rafe tore off his tie, and flipped open the top buttons of his shirt, the wiggling of Demi's hips causing small perspiration beads over his lip. He wiped them away impatiently. Nathaniel wasn't the only person who hadn't noticed Rafe's attempts at courtship, or the result of said courtship in a binding contract titled marriage.

"I love the rosebushes you brought. Just love them." Demi's voice came from inside the tepee.

"I thought we might go dancing tonight in Amen Flats. Maddy's Hot Spot has a band and—" Okay, Rafe frowned, so he had taken a poll of the Tallchief men, Alek and Joel to see what was available for dating purposes. Research in acquiring a project never hurt. Then there was that odd whimsical need to see her over a candlelight dinner, place that engagement ring on her finger and hold her in his arms, swaying to the music like everyone else. Rafe realized that he had never wanted to sway to music, lost in the scent and feel of his woman.

He wanted very much to have Demi. While she was winding her way through sly and flirtatious looks at him, a distinct change of her wardrobe from when he first met her, a certain swaying of her hips, and the long, scented baths in the upper level bathroom,

Rafe was—fragile, he decided again. He held onto a pole that had shifted dangerously.

"I love this idea..." Demi said from inside the tepee. "The Tallchiefs took a tip from their great-great-grandfather and each one has a bridal tepee. Did you know that each Tallchief has a cradle made by the Sioux chieftain to support his family? I love their legends—they all came true, and I can't wait for the meadow to be filled with their children. They're lovely, you know. Tons of black gleaming hair and beautiful, expressive gray eyes."

"Palladins always have green eyes," Rafe mentioned casually as he stuck out his foot to brace another shifting pole. If Demi wanted lovely children with him, they would have green eyes. "Ah, Demi, maybe you'd better come out."

"I'm busy in here. You can come inside in just a moment— Dancing? I'm sorry, I do not have experience."

"I used to be a fair dancer. I placed first in an all-night contest." He wanted to hold her close in his arms and sway to slow beats, nuzzling her hair, feel her soft thighs move against his— Rafe inhaled abruptly. He really wanted an all-night contest of another variety.

"I just love the Tallchiefs. I'm so glad we're related. You can come in now."

Rafe glanced at the shifting, unstable poles, the loose canvas draped haphazardly over the poles, shook his head and eased into the tepee.

Demi was seated on a blanket inside, holding cloth in her hands, her eyes glowing up at him. Rafe seated himself closely to her. "Palladin, Inc. could provide a good sturdy model for you. You could have a discount," he offered to avoid an argument similar to the appliance one.

"I can't wait. I want to invent my own tepee. Here." She eased the folded cloth into his hand. "For you."

In the shadows, Rafe held the fabric as if it would break. Excitement seemed to burst from Demi. "What is it?"

She laughed aloud, the sound enchanting him as she reached

to drape an arm around his neck, snuggling close. Rafe closed his eyes briefly, giving thanks to the dating god for Demi's new ease with him. Not that much ease, of course, his body reminded him, because in the middle of it all, he'd gone old-fashioned, desiring to have her when he was certain he wouldn't be Thomas's replacement. The acquiring process was taking more time than his nerves could stand.

The light green shirt in his hands was embroidered delicately, tiny bluebells spread from shoulder to shoulder, twined with darker blades of grass. "Green for your eyes," Demi whispered, kneeling beside him, her head on his shoulder. "Two bluebells for every night you were away from me. Those small, red buds near them are kisses."

"You made this for me?" Stunned, Rafe reeled amid his shifting uncertain tide of emotions. He traced the tiny red dots. "'Kisses,'" he said unevenly, and realized he was slightly lightheaded with whimsy.

"Just for you. I made you shorts, too. They match my Demi's Delites style, Stormy. The boxer kind—" Demi giggled as Rafe bore her to the blanket, the shirt crushed between them. The tepee collapsed upon them, gently enfolding them in a private, tender world.

"Thank you." He smoothed her cheek with his fingertips. "Exactly what does this mean, sweetheart?"

She lifted slightly to kiss him. "That you are a very special man."

Rafe waded through the implications, circled them, dispensed with the urge to take her quickly, hurry her off and propose marriage to her. He tossed the idea of the children into the mix along the way, and forced himself to breathe. "Thank you," he repeated humbly as his heart turned warm and fuzzy.

Demi's mysterious, shadowed look caused him to kiss her gently. She stirred restlessly beneath him, and with a purr, locked her arms around him, her hips gently inviting his, and the kiss turned into hunger....

Ten

"**D**emi, you come out of there this minute," a male voice ordered shrilly. "Nathaniel told me you were in the meadow, and I just heard you cry out feverishly. Are you hurt?"

"Someone is going to be hurt, if I get to him," Rafe promised darkly. He breathed raggedly, sucking in the scent of Demi's warm, moist, fragrant skin. His lips were poised in the delicious crevice between Demi's breasts, his body locked over hers, he trembled with the need to make them one. Demi's hand slid from the aching part of him that she was just beginning to timidly, intimately investigate. Rafe trembled with the desire to have her touch him. Their moments of intimacy were brief, shattering and usually interrupted by—almost anything, including his instincts to protect her from his raging desire.

"It's Thomas," she whispered desperately. In the shadows of the tepee, her eyes pled with Rafe.

Rafe clenched his body tight, restraining his passion and groaned. He eased from her. Demi's face paled; her fingertips dug into him. Rafe closed his eyes. She was ashamed to be with him; the old emotions from his youth dropped on him like stone. Suddenly he felt very old.

Demi reached for his hand and settled it over her breast. The small hard nub rested trustingly in his palm and eased his taut pain. Demi placed Rafe's other hand on her, pressing her hands over his. "Thomas will want to hurt you. He had karate lessons."

While Rafe tried to deal with his renewed desire, and Demi's mood shift from embarrassed to concern for his welfare, she frowned grimly. "I will protect you."

Rafe ran his thumbs over the hardened nubs of her breasts and groaned. "I thought the guy was remarried. Why do you think he might want to—"

He remembered the picture in the library: Thomas receiving a literary award from Nathaniel. Bookish and small, Thomas looked as athletic as a snail. Rafe's body shook as he forced himself not to chuckle. He doubted that Thomas had ever stepped into a back alley, bare-knuckle brawl and came away unscathed. Rafe tensed, fighting outright laughter.

Demi looked at him sharply. While he kept both hands locked to her breasts, unwilling to release her, she smoothed his hair, kissed his cheek and cuddled him. "You're trembling. Your whole body is shaking. I will not have you threatened. Don't be frightened."

Clearly his moment to intimately deliver had passed and Rafe regretted tucking her into the fragile silk bra. He firmly intended there to be another time to make love to her and to tell her that whatever happened between them, she had made him very happy. He smoothed the round softness, ran his fingertip under the shell-shaped lace for a lingering last temptation and reluctantly buttoned her blouse. "Why does he feel he has the right to—" He cleared that chuckle out of his throat. "To defend you?"

"He left Esmeralda and wants me back. He's written me several sonnets about souls being forever married. They were lovely. He's talented, and I have always been his reader and his editor.

He's all alone out there on the publishing frontiers now. I've offered to help him for a time—just to adjust.'' Demi began to crawl out of the fallen tepee, and stopped to pat his head. "Stay here, darling. I will protect you."

"He can't have you—" Rafe shook his head, trying to clear it. "'Darling',''' echoed sweetly. He grabbed her ankle as she began crawling out again. "What did you call me?"

"Darling.'' She sounded distracted and grim as she stood and stated briskly, "Well, Thomas. You've found me. Say your piece and then you may leave."

Rafe eased to his knees, holding the cloth and poles away from him. He tried to crawl out of the tepee and then simply stood, forcing the poles and fabric upright until he could step out. It collapsed behind him just as a red-faced, furious Thomas took a threatening step toward Demi.

While she seemed oblivious to danger, Rafe recognized the signals from experience. "I wouldn't,'' he advised too softly.

Thomas glanced at Rafe, who had lightly tossed the tepee aside, and took a step back. "Demi, I thought we were working on a reconciliation. Now I find you rolling with the hired help.''

He eyed Rafe. "He's big, isn't he? Neanderthals usually are...no brain, just brawn. But I was a grade school boxing champion. I'm going to teach him a lesson about meandering with my wife's affections in a language he can understand.''

"Now, that's an invitation.'' Rafe took a step forward and Demi's finger braced against his chest. He looked down at the slender tether and then into the steel gray of Demi's gaze.

"Do you love him?" he asked quietly and wondered if his heart had stopped beating as he waited for her answer. Only heartbeats ago, he had planned to circle Demi's feelings and ease her into a commitment, finalized by marriage. He had a list in his pocket of things he wanted to say to her, a carefully chosen list that would make him more appealing.

He'd wanted to give her the five hundred acres he'd just purchased, a portion of the old Tallchief lands. It was an outright gift with no obligations; he wanted her to have her heritage. As a man without legends and love in his background, he wanted the best for Demi. Now Rafe glared at Thomas, the intruder, and waited for Demi to answer him. Demi's thoughtful frown as she considered him and Thomas, each in turn, caused fear to slam into Rafe. He wondered briefly if there were anonymous sonnet writers he could hire to— He tossed the thought away; he wanted a true relationship and a commitment with Demi, and they weren't built on falsehoods. Impatience and desperation caused him to repeat, "Do you love him?"

"In a way, I do. I grew up with him and he was a part of my life for so many years. But in the other way, you know...that way... Would I be—you know—with you just a moment ago, if I did?" she demanded in an urgent whisper Thomas couldn't hear.

"So what does that mean?" Rafe watched impatiently as she slyly slipped a button he had missed into place.

"You really must see to that eyelid. It's twitching again." She reached to smooth his hair, which was standing out in peaks from his battle with the tepee. "It means you are the fairest of the lot, you...you...darling."

Rafe felt light-headed; he thought he just might swoon. "Fairest of the lot" and "Darling" rated much higher than chief of acquisitions and product development. He eyed Thomas, who glared back. If Demi thought of him as her darling, Rafe could afford to be generous. For Demi's sake, he would try to be friendly. "I understand you write sonnets?"

Thomas bristled. "Very good ones. You haven't a chance. My wife likes the intelligent mind."

"Your wife." Rafe's pleasant mood plopped into a fresh cowpile. He took a step forward, on his way to teach Thomas the fine technique of pasture brawling.

Demi's fingertip stopped him again. "Thomas, I insist that you not refer to me as your wife. Rafe has immense talents and he has helped me develop programs for my students. He's an excellent businessman. His help has been invaluable to the survival of my father's dream...and my own.''

Thomas squinted at Rafe. "I'd like to speak with you alone, Demi.''

"Very well. We do have business to discuss.'' Demi smiled hopefully up at Rafe. "Would you mind terribly?''

"Oh, well, hell, yes, I mind. You're marrying me and that's all there is to it. Dear Thomas can hire someone else to edit his lovely sonnets.''

Demi stiffened and Rafe recognized that pale, rigid expression, her stormy gray eyes narrowing. The fairest of the lot realized his mistake, but a mixture of pride and fear did not allow him to retreat.

"I have grown to like making my own choices, apart from the dire need to function and survive. Remember that, Mr. Palladin. Perhaps we could talk when you are calmer,'' Demi said between her teeth as they stared at each other.

"Sweetheart, I have never been more in control,'' Rafe shot back.

Control? He lost that the moment he met Demi, goddess of his harvest.

"I am not an acquisition,'' Demi said after a long, tense pause. "And I will not argue with you. Not here. Not now. I will not be forced to make decisions because two males decide that I must.''

Thomas smoothed his hair. "He's just using you to get the castle. It makes sense that he acquire you. You, of course, can't see the obvious.''

Demi pivoted to him. "What did you say, Thomas?''

"He's already purchased five hundred acres bordering your land. I checked property values at the local real estate office. With the potential that this castle has as a resort, he'd be a fool not to marry you. Don't think for a moment that he's hot for you alone. You are simply an obstacle to be—acquired—so that the Palladin empire can absorb the castle. Look at you...you're wearing a single braid, dangling down your front. It looks very heathenish.''

Demi turned slowly to Rafe. Her eyes were already shimmering with tears, condemning him. She looked back at Thomas and then turned to Rafe, her bottom lip trembling, her hands clasped tightly together. She studied him intensely, so long that Rafe knew she'd seen every dark deed he'd done before the Palladin brothers decided they wanted their pride. She looked at him as if seeing into his soul, as if measuring him to Thomas and Nathaniel.

She couldn't trust him. The evidence was stacked against him. "Darling" time was over; the game had been played and he'd lost.

In his lifetime, it hadn't mattered that others trust him, but now without Demi's trust—

Rafe straightened his shoulders, met her gaze and felt his dark, chilling shadows enfold him. An explanation would look as though he were caught in the act and trying to conceal it as a gift. *She didn't trust him.* His heart tore slightly, then half of it dropped away into the shadows. What did he expect? His dark legacy made him suspect for anything. Demi would have to decide for herself what she believed and from her pale expression, she believed the worst. Rafe took a deep breath. "Believe what you will."

"That land once belonged to the Tallchiefs. The castle is my father's dream, Rafe," Demi whispered unevenly, tears spilling over her lashes and streaming down her cheeks. She continued to stare at him as if seeing him for the dark invader that he was, the mercenary sent to grasp Dr. Valerian's dream.

"What did you expect, Demi?" Thomas continued brutally. He stopped talking and edged behind Demi when Rafe took a forward step. Rafe eased her aside, put his hand over Thomas's face and pushed him. Thomas sprawled into several fresh cowpiles.

He struggled to his feet, holding his damp slacks away from him. "Neanderthal."

The painful band around Rafe's chest tightened; he had once more proven that he was just one step above the brawling teenage hood he had fought to leave behind.

He nodded curtly, unable to speak, his throat tight with emotion.

Demi's hand stretched to his, taking it firmly. Her eyes continued to trace his face, finding his soul, opening it. Without looking at Thomas, she spoke to him. "I'm afraid I can no longer edit your sonnets, Thomas. The castle is my father's dream, but now I have found my own very dear dream, the man who fills my heart."

Thomas sputtered. "This...this caveman? Don't you see what he is? That he wants Valerian land? He has put a...a sex spell over you, Demi, and you are not thinking clearly. But then you never could. According to my research, there are herbs that can make a woman—"

"For the first time, I am thinking very clearly, about what I want." Demi's hand raised to smooth Rafe's cheek. "You may go now, Thomas. And by the way, sex is nice—heavenly—with the right person."

Rafe turned to kiss her palm; their gazes locked. "Am I in a dream?" he asked unsteadily, fearing that any moment he'd awake and find himself back in the shadows—without Demi.

Nathaniel hurried from the castle, carrying a suitcase. Prince and King bounded beside him, tongues happily dangling and big feet tangling. "Hello, Thomas," Nathaniel said cheerfully. "Sorry, I am leaving. B.J. just called. She needs me. She's found evidence of a new conquistador scroll." He flushed and tucked the tie and the feminine, lacy lingerie dangling from his suitcase into it.

Prince and King ran full speed to Thomas and knocked him back into the cowpiles. The huge pups licked his face while he fought to get to his feet.

A helicopter swooped over the mountains and Nick waved after he had landed. Nathaniel hurried across the meadow to it. Then he stopped and turned to Demi, as though asking her permission.

Demi stepped forward, threw out her arms and called. "I love you, Father. You didn't forget my Tiger Pretty set of briefs for B.J., did you? Give B.J. a big kiss for me."

Nathaniel caught the kiss she threw and grinned boyishly, while he tucked it into his pocket.

"They're getting married," Demi whispered and moved into Rafe's arms as the helicopter lifted and swung away. He enfolded her safely against him, where she should be, close to his heart. Demi looked up at him. "I'm so happy. You'll come to the wedding?"

"The wonderful B.J. is a lady, I take it?"

"She's even more of a scholar than Father is, but she is a very physical woman. He's acting like a boy. B.J. has a cat and now Father isn't allergic to animals anymore. It seems his allergies flare up when he's tense and he's not tense anymore. He's happy."

"What about me?" Thomas whined, bracing himself as the pups jumped against him.

Demi took the pups' collars and shushed them into sitting quietly at her feet. "If you write a sonnet to her, I am certain that Esmeralda will return to you."

"You'll be sorry," Thomas threw at her, stalking away to his battered car.

Demi placed her head on Rafe's shoulder as Thomas's car sputtered and died several times. "I suppose I'll have to start it for him—"

Rafe glanced at the dogs, pointed to them and ordered, "Stay." The dogs sat while he hurried to the car, lifted the hood, adjusted the choke, slammed the hood down and glared at Thomas. The car, belching oil fumes, rattled out of the valley.

"Now where were we?" he asked when he turned to see Demi smiling softly up at him, her hand lodged firmly in his belt.

"I was about to tell you about Elizabeth's legend, but—"

Rafe swung her up into his arms and started striding toward the castle, the pups leaping beside them. With any luck, he could make it upstairs to the bed he'd dreamed about Demi sleeping in—with him.

Rafe swept up the stairway, pausing to turn and order firmly, "Stay," to the pups, who stayed. Demi placed her lips upon his throat, nibbled on it and hugged him closely. He could look so stunned when she cuddled close to him. She began to unbutton his shirt, placing tiny kisses on his chest. Rafe stood absolutely still, holding her tightly, his body shivering, his eyes closed as if he were wallowing in something he wanted very much.

"The nice thing about you, is that you're very emotional," Demi whispered against his lips.

"I'm not feeling nice," he returned with a quick, hard kiss that left Demi reeling. She licked her lips, tasting his promise of passion and clutched his broad shoulders; he would keep her safe. She flexed her fingertips lightly, pressing into his muscled shoulder. She needed a man as strong as herself, as independent and as...passionate. She flexed her fingers again—and muscle and cord leaped beneath her touch. Demi smiled; Rafe was strong enough to equal what she had planned.

Rafe swept into the shadowy bedroom and kicked the door closed behind him. He carried her to the bed and kneeled upon the bed to gently lower her. He bent over her, freeing her braids, arranging the long rippling strands upon the black satin pillow. "I've dreamed of this flowing upon me, the scent of it—" he rasped deeply.

"Rafe?" She ached for him, needed to have his strength enfold her, lodge deeply within her, locking them together.

"I want to make this perfect, sweetheart. So that you'll know just who you belong to, and who belongs to you." He smiled softly and sat, drawing her legs across his lap. He began to tug off her fireman's boots. "You won't need these for a while. A long while."

"Wait—" The two boots plopped to the floor.

Rafe turned slowly to her, his hand running up and down the length of her thigh. "You've changed your mind," he stated warily.

Demi kneeled beside him, cradled his face in her hands and kissed him. "No. I want you very much."

He frowned. "I'm not handling this right. I have feelings for you, Demi, and maybe I'm pushing too hard. I need you. I'll probably always need you, but in different ways. Right now—"

"I know. Right now is very special. I need you, too."

His fingers tightened on her jean-clad thigh. "There's more than this— We can wait—"

She laughed outright and hugged him close, feeling the passion burn fever hot between them. "I can't wait."

He began to unbutton her blouse, slowly, replacing the buttons with kisses, his fingers trembling, his breath warm upon her skin. The soft restrained touches, a brush of his fingertips across her silk covered breasts, the stroke of his palm upon her femininity, gently massaging her, caused Demi to shiver and heat; her heart pounded to an uneven racing beat. His lips gently suckled, nibbled, cherished erotically over the lace, dampening it, peaking her aching nipples. "I can feel the fire in you," he whispered unevenly. "You're burning—"

"For you. Oh, Rafe—" His mouth took hers boldly, desperately, his tongue playing seductively with his. She locked her fingers in his hair, holding him close, trying to get closer.

Rafe tugged away her bra, the fine fabric tearing, his body shaking, and yet his callused hands ran so gently over her, like feathers, soothing, caressing, cherishing. His palm skimmed over her shoulder, slid slowly down her side and then his fingers closed possessively on the jut of her hip, drawing her firmly to him. "Are you certain this is what you want?"

"Yes, I need you now...." Demi fumbled with his belt buckle and Rafe ripped it away impatiently, placing her hands upon the warm, hard, muscled shield of his stomach. He tore his shirt away, his hands skimming her flesh, molding it gently, claiming her. The pulse of him flowed through her palms, as if he were throbbing, waiting just for her. He sucked in his breath as she gently slid his zipper downward.

Breathing unevenly, Rafe cupped her face, drawing her to him for another long, seductive, tender kiss that heated quickly, hungrily as his pants slid away. A quick movement tore her briefs free and they lay chest to breast, hardened desire waiting for a softer moist nest, hearts trembling, pulses racing.

Demi gently curled her fingers around his hardness and Rafe's uneven, desperate groan swept into the shadows. He tensed, shivering, and the wild hunger beneath his lowered lids answered the tearing demands coming deep from within her. She pressed close to delicately bite his shoulder, then lick the small wound and Rafe's body surged upward, filling her hand.

His big hands warmed her thighs, stroking them, rocking her gently to him. With a shudder, Rafe eased over her, bracing his weight from her, his body trembling. He moved his chest, side to side, a luxurious caress to her sensitive, aching breasts. Then as she gathered him to her, locking her arms and legs around him to complete the bond she felt already with him, Rafe found her and pushed slowly, firmly inside her. Their eyes met and locked, a promise given and taken, their hands joined on the pillow by her head. He filled her fully, releasing the pleasured cry that had been building within her.

She fought him; she clung to him and always there was the sense of coming home, coming to the final peace, working together and knowing that they would be complete. That they were building passion and a bond, forging it from heat and storms and tenderness. This was the man who had her heart, stroking her, making her one with him, going so deeply that there would never be doubt that they had bonded physically. The heat rose, throbbed within her as Rafe suckled her breasts, their bodies moving fluidly together as if they were always meant to be. Rafe's hand slid beneath her hips, lifting her against him.

Higher rose the fever; Demi cried out as her body clenched rhythmically, tightly around Rafe. He would always keep her safe; there would be more, deeper, and— The pleasure came surging, burning, higher and higher, faster and faster, and a final burst hurled her even higher. There, with Rafe's face above her, his expression fierce and possessive as she wanted, Demi clung to him, staring up at him as their bodies finalized the deepest bond, pledging their hearts, their lives to become one.

On that plane, covered with mist and flowers and sunshine, with Rafe's body joined deeply with hers, his fiery stare devouring her just as she fed upon him, there would be more, always more, more than these fevered moments, when their hearts and bodies joined, linked, mated forever.

He was a part of her, just as she was his.

They loved.

They were no longer separates, but joined, forged together, filling each other.

"Demi, Demi, Demi..." Rafe whispered desperately as his body hardened, tensed and poured into hers.

For a time, the heat easing, Rafe held himself poised above her, his green gaze soft upon her as if he'd remember her always, lying this way—her hair spread out upon the pillow. He slowly wound the strands around his fingers, studied them, then looked slowly, heavily at her, emotions flickering beneath his lashes.

His body relaxed, and Demi eased him upon her, slowly enfolding him with a sense of peace that the moment was perfect. She was where she belonged—in Rafe's arms. She smoothed his back, gentling him and Rafe's hot face nuzzled her shoulder, his arms still locked around her, his hands opened and possessive upon her, stroking her gently, soothing her. This was the gentleness that always rode beneath their passion, that melded them together. He was as much hers now as he was when the passion drove him and she knew it would always be. "Don't go."

His lashes fluttered against her throat. "I'm heavy."

"You sprawl lightly." Demi lost herself in the pleasure of his warm, muscled weight, the wonderful lazy ease after the storms.

Rafe closed his eyes and Demi sensed him drawing away from her, pain shadowing the rugged contours of his face. "I didn't mean to take you so roughly. I promise—"

"Shh. I wanted you just as desperately. I was beginning to wonder if you always had control—"

His kiss stopped her. "I used to. You've changed that. You bloom like a rose when you're making love, the petals first holding me tight and tender, then full and curling and taking me deeper. You fill me with your scent, the sounds you make—drowsy, hungry, desperate little purrs of pleasure and then the heat pours out of you like warm, dewy silk. You move in waves, completing me, holding me, cherishing me. You give to me and we become a part of each other in more than our bodies."

"You feel like that?" she asked, amazed that he would share his intimate thoughts with her.

She blinked, feeling him surge strongly within her. Her body clenched immediately, claiming him. With a wicked, enchanting laugh, Rafe eased to one side and drew her over him. He spanned her stomach with his hand, his fingers sliding lower and the moment he touched her, she began to burst, layer by heated layer. The fierce rhythm caught her the moment his lips touched her breasts, heated cords running feverishly, throbbing, down to the very center of her.

Fifteen minutes or a century later, Demi's hand flopped from Rafe's chest. He smoothed the warm scented flesh flowing softly against him and circled her waist to draw her closer in his room's rumpled, shadowy bed. Her lashes fluttered and Rafe watched with delight as Demi licked her kiss-swollen lips and opened her drowsy eyes. "Goodness," she whispered huskily, the heated, racing tempo of their lovemaking still threading her tone.

Rafe chuckled and enjoyed the slow, caressing stroke of her soft thigh against his. Their desire had been feverish, fast and momentarily eased his driving need to take her slowly, thoroughly. "Tell me what just happened, Demi?"

Her lips curled smugly. "Oh, I think you know. I didn't know men shouted there at the end. Though not loud, it came so raw and passionate, as if everything you were and would be came pouring out of you."

He'd wanted to make a child with her. The need rose, erupted from him unexpectedly, fierce, primitive and ultimate. His release had come too quickly, startling him, and Rafe had been unable to withhold his shattering emotions. It was as if the universe had opened to him and all the beautiful magic of the world poured into his heart. When Demi's body began gloving his rhythmically, he'd powered desperately right to the finish line and now he was dazed, uneasy with how she would think of him. It was very important that Demi know she was cherished, not used. He determined that the next time they made love, which would be within moments, that he would move more slowly, explaining his heart to her. He smoothed her thigh and found himself blushing. His shout of release and pleasure echoed in the shadows, mocking him. "That was a first for me."

Demi nuzzled his chest, her tongue flicking out to taste him. "You mean you've never—ever?"

"Never...ever. You came to me too fast." He glanced around at the clothing strewn on the floor and across the bed. Rafe scooped up her briefs and her torn bra. The torn strap dangled from the lace, proof of his urgency. "I've never done that before, either. I've never been that desperate. I've never felt like a revved-up teenage boy, not even when I was young. But I do around you. On the other hand, I've never felt more like a man."

Demi circled his lips with her fingertip. "But I like you desperate, as if nothing could stop you from me. And you certainly are all man."

"I'd stop for you, if it killed me." Rafe pulled the black satin sheet up to Demi's shoulder. He tugged it down, kissed her

gleaming fragrant shoulder and covered her again. "I wasn't prepared to—"

"To withhold your emotions. You were so desperate, trying
magnificently to be patient—such a valiant effort to make certain
you handled me gently, as if fearing you would hurt me. I knew
you would take care to see that my needs were met...and I knew
I couldn't wait. I—I forgot about everything but you. My goodness, Rafe—two times. Two times," she repeated in a dazed tone.
"I am a greedy woman."

Rafe allowed himself a full, class-A smirk. After all, he was
floating in petals, wallowing in dreams. "Am I back to the 'darling' stage?"

She snorted delicately, enchanting him. Rafe tipped her chin
up with his fingertip. "Tell me what just happened in the
meadow."

Beneath the sheet, Demi's foot stroked his. "I knew you'd ask.
You're methodical, and much too good at logic to skip that moment. It was all very simple once Thomas and you stood side by
side in the meadow. Two very different men, one selfish and one
sweet—that one was you. It came to me that you've always supported my independence—Palladin's chief of acquisitions and
product development had much more important things to do than
folding brochures to help me. You've never said anything negative about my ideas, merely adding tips to shape them into better
ones. You didn't ask that my life revolve around yours, rather
you gave me mine. You're a strong man, Rafe, but you give and
you recognize the importance of other people's lives. You could
have torn my father's dream away at any time, but you didn't.
You only made it better. I knew that you wanted to please
me...that the land was meant in some way to please me, as a part
of my inheritance."

She braced her arm on his chest and ran her fingers along his
face, as though memorizing his features. "I stood there in the
sunlight and realized suddenly, that I had my dreams. My very
own dreams, apart from what was expected of me. I had achieved

my goals to put the castle on a paying basis, but meanwhile I saw that I wanted more from life. I wanted to see you walk to me—well, you seem to prowl toward me with a dangerous pirate look in your green eyes as if I am just what you want. That pleases me. It pleases me when you hold my hand, and you can be so sweet. I've never had a wildflower bouquet before. You took time to stop and pick perfect wildflowers, each with exactly the same stem length.''

"I'm sweet?" The revelation stunned Rafe. "Exactly how?"

"The little things you do. Like stirring soup when it needs it. Like folding towels when I'm rushing around. The small things that matter. And there's that way you fold me against you at times. It's like you've found peace with me and I know I can always depend on you, even in the worst storms.''

Demi lifted the leg Rafe was stroking and studied her toe ring. "My body goes through a whole series of changes when you are near and I feel complete. Not just now, but when you are with me.''

She turned to him, her expression soft and tender. "I feel like a woman should feel—vibrant, cherished, and that is even when we are arguing, which I've never done before. When we argue, it's like a raging tempest that I know will always settle just right. You may try to bully me, but never harm me. You purely enjoy the challenge, but you would never shove aside my wishes. Oh, you're stubborn, not manageable at all and you've got this compulsive need to acquire me. I thought I would never marry again, to serve someone else—in fact, that terrified me. Then there's Elizabeth's legend. With you, I feel more like we...''

"We belong together," he offered huskily, his heart opening, warming, softening.

Her silky hair fell over him, the fragrance enticing him, as she leaned closer. "You are my dream, Rafe.''

"I'm your darling," he corrected smugly with a long, promising kiss.

Demi snuggled close to Rafe, aware that he was not sleeping. In the quiet shadows, with the castle settling for the night, she was where she wanted to be every night for the rest of her life. The midnight snack he'd brought up to their bed had been devoured between kisses and tickling and laughter; she'd experienced her first thorough Rafe-bath, and once again passion had destroyed her plans to talk quietly with him. She knew his troubled past, his unknown birth mother, still troubled him. She stroked his chest. "Yes?"

In the shadows of night, he arched an eyebrow and looked down at her. His hand closed firmly, possessively over her hip; his thumb slowly caressed her skin. With his hair rumpled and the tension on his face eased, Rafe smiled lightly. "I didn't say anything."

Demi sat up, tugged the satin sheet to her well-seduced, slightly aching breasts and asked, "But something is bothering you. What is it?"

Terror shot through her. Rafe was not ready to share his thoughts with her and what if…what if she had stepped over some unknown relationship line? What if she had revealed everything of her heart, frightening him?

"We're getting married, of course," he stated flatly, as though dismissing an unimportant fact in pursuit of more important ones.

Demi did not want to test the way he served that fact to her. She trusted Rafe to know that she needed a more gentle and rounded invitation into a lifetime commitment.

His hand curled around her knee, his thumb stroking the inner flesh. "Okay. What's the legend? I know it is important to you, just the way the Tallchiefs' legends are treasured. If I'm going to handle all this sweet business properly—and I intend to—I need to understand what pleases you. What is Elizabeth's legend?"

Demi knew that Rafe wanted her to be happy and that he wanted to understand. There would be times that they would battle—mmm, arguing with Rafe was energizing, thrilling, vibrant—because underneath, he cared and would not hurt her. "Look," she whispered, reaching to place the crystal Rafe had given her precisely onto the broken stem of Elizabeth's crystal.

"The edges fit," Rafe murmured, as the crystals glowed in the shadowy light. He looked at her and a tender bond ran between them, humming in the shadows. "Like we do."

"Exactly. Elizabeth said it was a new legend, one she created because of her love for Liam. She wrote the legend and placed it in the sword grip for another woman to share—*'Twil be the knight who brings his lady to this cave with clusters of crystals about— aye, the sparkling crystals shall shoot their cloak of colors about him, who loves her already. Rogue that he is, the lady will come to love him with all her heart.'*

Rafe's eyes glowed in the shadows, brilliant upon her. "We went to the cave that day and you— Do you?" he demanded, flatly, his body tensing as if to take a blow.

She raised his hand to her lips, placing a kiss in his callused palm. "Love you? Aye, I do," she whispered, borrowing a word from a woman who had loved just as deeply, all those years ago.

He trembled, placing his hands around her face and drawing her down to him for a long, tender kiss. His slightly rough fingertips smoothed her cheek and she knew that the shadows had eased within Rafe, that she gave him peace, and that he gave her love, though his lips were not yet ready for the new words. It was enough to find it in his dark emerald green gaze, in his touch and the brushing commitment of his lips....

Eleven

Rafe stood on the porch of a well-tended, old-fashioned, two-story home in Denver. Children's toys littered the fenced yard behind the house, a tire swing waiting to play. Above the shade trees, July's sky was clear, the mountains in the hazy distance. He crushed the small, worn scrap of paper in his hand. His birth mother's telephone number was burned into his mind; Demi had given it to him with a kiss, an expression of love and concern. "I love you. Aye, I do. These decisions are up to you," she'd whispered and cuddled closer to protect him from his fears.

Demi had left the rest to him. Their wedding would be in August and Rafe wanted to meet his storms, coming to Demi with his heart cleared of shadows.

He inhaled sharply, the fear that he might remind Julie Monroe too much of a man who had hurt her—Rafe's father. Rafe ran his hand across his jaw wearily. He couldn't help inheriting his father's looks and body build; he prayed he wouldn't terrify her at first sight. Rafe wasn't certain if he could take his newly found mother recoiling from the sight of him.

He had changed, softened and strengthened at the same time. Life with Demi had surprised Rafe; he was a gentle, loving man, unlike his father. Rafe wanted to tend the children he hoped they would have...hold them, love them.

Julie. That was his mother's name, and she wanted to see him. He pushed the doorbell and held his breath.

The door slowly opened to a tall, stately woman with clear, untroubled eyes. "Rafe..." The sound was soft, loving, tender.

She traced his features, so like his father's, and Rafe stiffened, waiting for her to recoil. Instead her hand touched his arm. "I've waited for you...my own dear firstborn son. A part of me has never rested, aching for you. I was afraid you would hate me for giving you to Belinda, but at the time, I was just fourteen and my parents—"

"I know. I'm sorry," Rafe managed to say unevenly as tears shimmered in Julie's eyes.

"Belinda loved you very much. For that year and a half before she died, she sent me letters about how strong and intelligent you were, such a nice boy. And then the letters stopped. I almost came to you then, but I was still a teenager and afraid of Lloyd, what he might do to my family. You were never out of my thoughts."

A tiny blond girl burst from the shadows and clung to Julie's knees. "Grandma?"

"This is May, your sister's little girl. May is staying with me while her mother works. You have two sisters, Rafe. I've told them about you. Would you like to meet them?" Julie's fears rode in her trembling tone. "Do you forgive me?" she asked suddenly.

"You're my mother," Rafe said simply, and felt the wounds healing as he looked at her, the past settling, replaced by a new life. "I want you and my...sisters to come to my wedding. It's at a castle in Wyoming, and the whole family will be there."

"Come in. We have so much to talk about...my son," Julie added softly, proudly, as she drew him into her home.

A slightly balding tall man placed his arm around her shoulders and shook Rafe's hand. "I'm George, her husband. She insists on manners, but today she's a little—"

Julie wiped tears from her eyes. "Happy. I am happy. Today, my son has come home."

"She's saved every article she could find about you. I'm glad you came."

Rafe inhaled slowly, trying to control the warmth filling his heart. Then he grinned, opening himself to happiness and the future. "My fiancée and I want you to come to our wedding. If you could, it would mean a great deal to us."

Demi could have put her hands around Rafe's muscled neck and squeezed slowly.

She kicked her long, lace wedding gown impatiently as the Tallchief women circled her, adjusting the pearl-and-flower headpiece. They tugged the veil down to cover her face. "We could have been married simply, by a justice of the peace," Demi muttered. "But, oh, no...Rafe was determined to fill the castle with friends and relatives...he wanted his brothers standing beside him and the Tallchiefs, and he wanted all of my family here with me. The Palladins look so much alike, I'll probably marry the wrong one."

"I don't think so, dear," Sybil murmured. "Rafe will be the one who watches you like a hawk about to swoop...or a groom about to carry you off."

"Oh, he would do that, wouldn't he?" Demi worried. Rafe's tendency to carry her off was only exceeded by his need to kiss her. "All very *proper* kisses," she muttered darkly, resenting his oldfashioned behavior, saving their love for their wedding night.

She took the bouquet of wildflowers, herbs and white roses from Elspeth. "You know he's planned this whole affair...rather he engineered it, from the flower and herb decked hallway to the banquet later and the grand waltz. A grand waltz...I have never waltzed. We had to practice. For some reason, he still can't stand to be in the car when I drive, yet when we dance, we fit perfectly. He's controlling...he's—"

"Rafe loves you. He wanted to see that you weren't too tired," Talia noted. "He'll settle down. Men are delicate, you know."

"He's so nurturing. He's so scheduled— He wanted to see that I wasn't too tired? Why?" Demi asked.

"Gee. Duh. Why would a groom want to make certain his bride isn't too tired on their wedding day?" Lacey asked with a grin.

Demi's veil shielded her blush. She had plans to use her excess energy with Rafe. "I love him."

"Aye, you do," the Tallchief women agreed at once, using their Scottish great-great-grandmother's vow.

"This wedding is his sonnet to me," Demi whispered and knew it was true—the beauty Rafe had created was a celebration for her alone; she mattered above all others in his life.

"Aye," the women agreed again, hugging her.

Demi stood at her father's side in the meadow, the Tallchiefs' tepees white against the lush green field. After hours of eating and dancing, late afternoon spread shadows from the mountains behind the castle. This ceremony was for the Tallchief and Palladin families, gathered close together, their tired children snuggling close or sleeping safely in the tepees.

Rafe herded sheep into the valley, a lone rider, dressed in his Western hat, the light green embroidered shirt, jeans and boots. His worn chaps gleamed in the late-afternoon shadows, a contrast to Roy's chestnut color. The Appaloosa mare tethered to his saddle horn was saddled.

Sheep moved in front of him as Rafe rode across the meadow, shadowed with mountains and pines, the clear sky still blue above. The small flock was a symbol of Rafe's paying a bridal price to her father. The sheep would remain on Tallchief lands; though Nathaniel had made plans to move to Arizona with B.J., Demi knew her cousins would help her learn to tend for the animals, to shear them for weaving wool. Yet the flock was a traditional statement that Rafe would care for her needs, cherish her above his own needs. She would weave and clothe him with their wool.

Demi straightened, her heart filled with happiness. Rafe was her future, her love. His pride meant as much to her as her own, and he wanted to give her this special gift, a traditional Tallchief ceremony.

She glanced at her father, who looked years younger and very healthy. This traditional ceremony pleased Nathaniel; he seemed to glow as he held his new wife's hand. Julie, Rafe's mother, stood near and Demi reached to squeeze the older woman's hand. They shared a look that promised their lives would blend together, loving the man between them. Mamie came to Julie's side and hugged her; the caring hug ran from grandmother to mother to bride.

Demi smoothed the wide Celtic wedding band Rafe had chosen for her, a symbol of her Scots heritage from the bride captured by Tallchief. She shivered, remembering how strongly Rafe spoke his vows, how green his eyes were before he kissed his new bride.

Her heart leaped at the sight of him and the joy he brought her.

She stood very still and proud as Rafe swung down from his saddle, his gaze locking with hers. He removed his hat, and placed it over the saddle horn and those green eyes never left her, his face hard with promise. Oh, there was nothing sweet and tender about him now, for he had come to claim her. Fierce pride rose in Demi, not the tender feelings of a bride about to start a new life, but a strong passion for the man already bonded to her in heart and body.

The evening breeze caught her loose hair; it flowed gently to one side, the ends licking at her waist. She wanted to come to Rafe this way, still dressed in her bridal gown, her hair free as he liked, glistening like rippling blue-black silk.

He walked to her slowly, carrying a leather pouch on his hip and leading the mare with his other hand. The wind riffled his hair and Demi's heart raced. This man was the other half of her heart; he was her love.

Rafe's gaze swung to Nathaniel's; the two men who shared her life silently agreeing in ancient male tradition that Demi would move from her father's keeping into Rafe's. Demi struggled against the tightening of her throat, the fear rising— Could she be all that he wanted, that he deserved? Would she fail him? She had one failed marriage behind her—

Rafe glanced at her and his look told her of his love and of his pride. She was what he wanted, more than worldly goods, dismissing his dark legacy to build a new one with her. They would live here, at the castle, and she would continue her business. Rafe would have an office from which to handle Palladin affairs. A foreman would be hired to take over the Palladin ranch duties, because Rafe intended to build a ranch with the five hundred Tallchief acres.

Demi smoothed the skirt of her gown, finding the small crystal tucked inside her garter. *'Twil be the knight who brings his lady to this cave with clusters of crystals about—aye, the sparkling crystals shall shoot their cloak of colors about him, who loves her already. Rogue that he is, the lady will come to love him with all her heart.*

Rafe placed the reins of the mare in Demi's hands. "Her name is Maud. She's gentle and has a strong, loving heart, like you."

Demi trembled as their hands met, clung and slid away. Rafe's gold wedding band, matching hers, gleamed upon his dark skin. In just that heartbeat, she knew how desperately Rafe wanted her, that the fires were controlled, for the moment—but now there was his pride to tend, and hers.

"Do you love me?" she asked, needing to keep her own pride on her wedding day.

"Yes. I love you." The answer was given unevenly, raw and primitive and straight from his heart. His eyes glowed upon her, the truth of his love running fiercely between them.

She nodded, accepting both gifts, their love to last forever.

Rafe placed the large leather bag on the grass and withdrew beaded moccasins, kneeling to remove her wedding slippers. He slid the moccasins onto her feet, his fingers briefly caressed her leg. His trembling touch told her that he was not as calm and controlled as he appeared. Rafe stood with the leather bag; it slid free and dropped at his feet.

He held a Tallchief cradle out to her. Hewn of one wooden piece, the cradle had been created long ago by Tallchief, a man providing for his family, selling his crafts.

Demi ran her fingers over the smooth, aged wood, which had been refinished. She fought the trembling of her lips, the tears of joy, burning at her lids. "Yes," she whispered, aching to hold his green-eyed baby in her arms. "I would like that."

Rafe handed the cradle to Nathaniel and lifted Demi high against his chest. He kissed her once—hard and brief and laden with promises he would keep; then placed her upon Maud.

In a lithe movement, Rafe swung up onto his saddle, and taking Maud's reins began to ride away from the meadow filled with Tallchief tepees.

Demi glanced at their families, emotions written on every face. She didn't wave; there would be other times. Now she looked at her new husband, riding straight and proud, ahead of her.

Her senses told her that tonight they would share their own bridal tepee and that Rafe would never be more tender, more bold, and that by morning, he would have told her more of his love.

"...about him, who loves her already. Rogue that he is, the lady will come to love him with all her heart."

Rafe gathered Demi to him at dawn, the echoes of her last cry filling the tepee. She gave him delight; she gave him peace, a sense of homecoming. She snuggled to him now, nuzzling his chest with her nose. She gathered him close to her, as if to keep him safe.

"I love you," he whispered, testing the new words on this first morning of their marriage. He intended to speak them every day, many times between dawn and sleep, to show his bride how much he cherished her.

Rafe smiled into Demi's flowing, scented hair and cuddled her closer—his wife, his heart, his love. He was home.

"Now, Rafe, please don't swoon," Demi pleaded two weeks later. She bent over him, clearly worried. "Darling?"

Rafe flattened himself to the blanket they were sharing on the starlit meadow. He needed the solid ground beneath him, or he'd go floating up into the night sky. He felt weak, happy, delighted, frightened and joyous.

"I feel fragile," he admitted when he could speak, because Demi loved to share their emotions. He flattened his hand over Demi's stomach. "This is the best— How do you know? Are you sure?"

"I knew on our wedding night. You were so—so virile and that marvelous muffled shout told me that you'd given your best to me— that you'd given me a child. I knew you'd go all soft and fuzzy when I told you. You're so sweet, when you're not trying to organize me."

"I'm finding that this marriage business is a two-way street. You do some pushing of your own."

She smiled smugly. "Yes. You need that, to keep you in line. I'd like to return the sword grip and the legend to the crystal cave—for another woman to find. It isn't every day you find a man who fills the legend of the crystal cloak. And, darling, you really fill my life."

"I love you," Rafe murmured, drawing her down to him. "Sometimes, I think I've loved you all my life."

"...him, who loves her already. Rogue that he is, the lady will come to love him with all her heart."

* * * * *

Look for Cait London's next book,
THE PERFECT FIT,
part of THE TALLCHIEFS *miniseries*
and Silhouette Desire's
MAN OF THE MONTH *selection,*
coming in December,
only from Silhouette Desire.

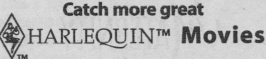

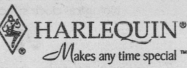

Coming September 1998

Three delightful stories about the blessings
and surprises of "Labor" Day.

TABLOID BABY by Candace Camp

She was whisked to the hospital in the nick of time....

THE NINE-MONTH KNIGHT
by Cait London

A down-on-her-luck secretary is experiencing
odd little midnight cravings....

THE PATERNITY TEST by Sherryl Woods

The stick turned blue before her
biological clock struck twelve....

*These three special women are very pregnant...and very
single, although they won't be either for too much longer,
because baby—and Daddy—are on their way!*

Available at your favorite retail outlet.

Look us up on-line at: http://www.romance.net   PSMATLEV

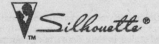

SILHOUETTE® Desire®

COMING NEXT MONTH

#1165 THE LONE TEXAN—Lass Small
The Keepers of Texas/50th Book

Tom Keeper, September's *Man of the Month*, had hung up his marriage hat, but he sure as heck hadn't given up that "one thing." And this stubborn bachelor was planning on showing prim beauty Ellen Simpson a thing—or two! Now, sweet Ellen would never let a cowboy wear his boots in her bedroom, but she absolutely insisted he keep his *hat* on....

#1166 MILLIONAIRE DAD—Leanne Banks
The Rulebreakers

Super-wealthy Joe Caruthers had been with plenty of women who couldn't keep their hands off him—or his checkbook. So when sensuous Marley Fuller became pregnant, he smelled a husband trap. Joe would never abandon his child, but he didn't have to become a husband to be a daddy...did he?

#1167 THE LITTLEST MARINE—Maureen Child
The Bachelor Battalion

After one passionate night with U.S. Marine Harding Casey, Elizabeth Stone found herself battling a fierce infatuation—and morning sickness—just days before he was set to sail overseas. Elizabeth knew honor and duty would bring Harding back, but she wanted him to return not just for his baby...but for his *wife*.

#1168 A SPARKLE IN THE COWBOY'S EYES—Peggy Moreland
Texas Brides

Merideth McCloud loved every moment of caring for John Lee Carter's darlin' baby girl. But it was high time the ornery bachelor learned that all those early-morning feedings—and late-night seductions—could lead only to one thing...marriage!

#1169 MIRANDA'S OUTLAW—Katherine Garbera

Luke Romero's rough-edged loner reputation was hard earned, and he intended to keep it intact. Then innocent Miranda Colby settled herself on *his* remote mountaintop. If Luke didn't shoo her off his territory soon, this virgin was in for a slight change to *her* reputation....

#1170 THE TEXAS RANGER AND THE TEMPTING TWIN—Pamela Ingrahm

Rough and tumble Quinn O'Byrne was straitlaced Kerstin Lundquist's secret desire...and her only hope at saving her twin. To her, he looked like any other leather-clad outlaw in Hell, Texas, but Quinn was actually an undercover lawman, bound for revenge. Was he also bound to risk everything...and fall in love?